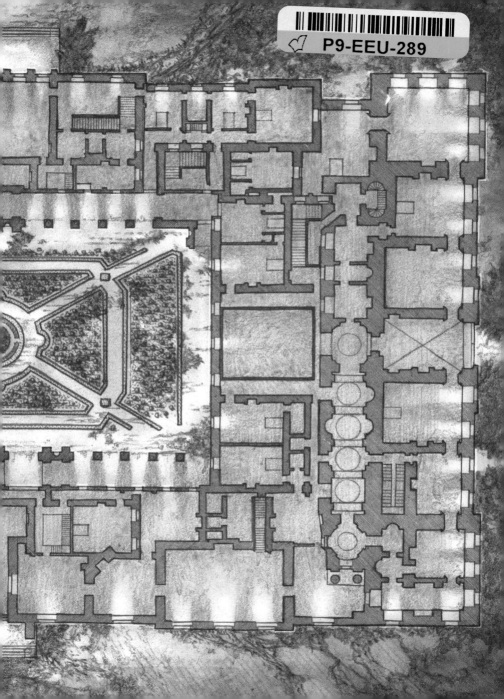

# WITHERWOOD
## REFORM SCHOOL

BOOK 1

# WITHERWOOD
# REFORM SCHOOL

## OBERT SKYE

WITH ILLUSTRATIONS BY
### KEITH THOMPSON

Christy Ottaviano Books

Henry Holt and Company ✝ New York

*To you, the reader—good luck!*

Henry Holt and Company, LLC
*Publishers since 1866*
175 Fifth Avenue
New York, New York 10010
mackids.com

Library of Congress Cataloging-in-Publication Data
Skye, Obert.
Witherwood Reform School / Obert Skye ;
with illustrations by Keith Thompson. — First edition.
pages       cm
"Christy Ottaviano Books."
Summary: "Siblings Charlotte and Tobias are trapped within a creepy reform school—and
entangled in its dark secrets"—Provided by publisher.
ISBN 978-0-8050-9879-2 (hardback) — ISBN 978-1-250-07347-1 (paperback)
ISBN 978-1-62779-320-9 (ebook)
[1. Brothers and sisters—Fiction.   2. Reformatories—Fiction.   3. Schools—Fiction.
4. Brainwashing—Fiction.]   I. Thompson, Keith, 1982– illustrator.   II. Title.
PZ7.S62877Wi 2015        [Fic]—dc23        2014041797

Henry Holt books may be purchased for business or promotional use.
For information on bulk purchases, please contact the Macmillan Corporate
and Premium Sales Department at (800) 221-7945 x5442
or by e-mail at specialmarkets@macmillan.com.

First Edition—2015 / Book designed by Véronique Lefèvre Sweet
Printed in the United States of America by R. R. Donnelley & Sons Company,
Harrisonburg, Virginia

1   3   5   7   9   10   8   6   4   2

YOU WILL BE CHANGED.

# DEAR READER

I wish I could tell you that life is made up of nothing but sunshine and kittens—how cute and warm that would be—but I've a feeling you already know that's not the case. You're clearly smart enough to understand that on certain days bad things happen. And by bad things, I don't mean stubbed toes or scraped elbows; I'm talking about things well worth fearing. Yes, fire can burn you, and poison may kill. But are you aware that sometimes great tragedy can come from something as simple as not holding your breath at the right time, or widening your eyes when the moment calls for them to be shut tight? I now know that whole histories can be changed, and lives can be burdened forever, by the simple misuse of a gravy boat. How do I know this? Well, let's just say I know the Eggers children, and I'm painfully aware of what they are going through. May you find more hope than abhorrence in their tale.

Yours in either case,
*Obert Skye*

# A Giant Seed

*Some prologues are just for show, bits of writing that come at the beginning of books directly before the good stuff. If you're like me, you might not care for them. You probably wish they'd just get to the story already, dive right into chapter one. I understand, but I want to assure you that this prologue is important—it's also not that long. And whereas I don't wish to be the kind of person who tells you what to do, I suggest you read it.*

There is a very old desert not too far away from where you now sit, stand, lie, or lean. It's as wide as a great lake and as empty as the parking lot of a long-abandoned mall. If you squint hard enough, you can see purple-tinted mountains off to the west. No need to squint while looking the other direction, because all that's there is desert—dusty land that appears to simply run off into the horizon like a dry river that has no end and no beginning.

Thousands of years ago, something happened in this desert—something unusual. It began as a normal day, but as the afternoon descended, the once-clear sky became overcast. Gray clouds moved in, causing the sky to look like a thick soup filled with dark mushy potatoes and noodles of twisting sunshine. Those noodles reached down and poked bits of the land, where weeds grew in the fashion of unwanted hair on the earth's dusty back.

As the lonely desert lay blanketed in gray, an object deep in space hurtled toward the earth at a remarkable speed. Rodents and insects living on the soil looked up in surprise as the air filled with the sound of a massive meteor screaming toward them. The meteor broke through the earth's atmosphere, creating a boom that mimicked a billion sheets of glass shattering against a metal floor. The boom was followed by a whistle. Three seconds later, the meteorite smacked against the soil in the middle of the desert. It was no ordinary smack—it was the kind of smack that steals every bit of your breath and leaves you feeling sick and unsettled for weeks to come.

A massive ring of dust and smoke shot into the swirling sky. Dozens of birds collided in the air and fell to the earth. It was very dramatic and awesome, not in the sense of a cool new shirt or a particularly great song, but awesome like two planets colliding.

The ground settled, and the gray clouds above exhaled and spread out slowly. A light rain began to fall, and the desert calmed. For a moment things looked as they always had. The only difference was that where the meteorite had slammed down, there was now a wide, hissing hole in the earth.

The new hole gurgled and spit. It widened, and dirt shot out like a filthy fountain. The winds intensified, and the hole quickly began to suck the soil back down into itself.

The rain increased.

Rocks and dirt flew in from all directions, drawn to the buried meteorite. In a few moments, there was a mound of soil big enough to be called a hill. The mound burped, sending dirt up and out into the wet air like muddy vines. Waves of wet soil rolled across the desert, washing up against the hill and pushing it higher and higher. Boulders the size of cars tore loose from the ground and flew in.

The smaller waves of soil were followed by a tsunami of land from the east. It thundered in and engulfed the hill, packing the earth and quickly making it hundreds of feet higher. Soil twisted and rolled from the bottom to the top, giving the hill a surface as level as any respectable table. The soil still blowing fell to the earth with a great *harrumph!* And then the rain stopped.

The purple-tinted mountains in the distance had not moved, but the desert was no longer empty. Where there was once nothing, now there sat a towering mesa hundreds of feet high. It had three steep sides and a sloping back, and it stuck up from the flat land like a blocky thumb. The birds that had fallen to the ground shook it off and took to the sky once more, acting as if a meteorite had not just come to earth and created a lonely mesa that would remain empty for thousands of years. Until the day when some well-meaning travelers would discover it and one of them would have the bright idea to build a school on top of it.

# CHAPTER 1

# LUMPY GRAVY

**T**obias Eggers looked at his sister, Charlotte, as they sat at the dinner table with their nanny. He breathed out slowly and nodded. It wasn't the kind of nod one civil grown-up would give another grown-up as they passed on the sidewalk. Nor was it the sort of nod you might use when someone asks if you would like a piece of cake. Nope, it was the kind of nod that only a mischievous child could execute. Charlotte nodded back, her hands shaking slightly.

Tobias patted the object hidden in the front pocket of his red hoodie. He reached up to the back of his head and squeezed a handful of his dark brown hair—a habit he had had ever since he was a little kid. The top of his hair stuck up slightly, and his shoulders were wide, making him appear much more athletic than he actually was. Tobias was smart and good with his hands. It was not unusual to find him taking apart locks and machines to see how they worked, or to find him with a pencil in hand drawing maps and making lists. If he had been making a list at the moment, item number one would have read *Get back at Martha*.

Tobias glanced across the table and focused on their nanny. Martha Childress was a large woman who was currently groaning and mumbling as she shoveled food into her face. She had a fork in one hand and a spoon in the other, and she was whirling potatoes and meat into her mouth like a buzz saw. She was wearing the same brown blouse and same boring blue skirt she always did. She was also wearing a plain white apron. It looked like the employee uniform of a store called Dull. Her sensible black shoes knocked against the legs of the table and made everyone's plate shake. Martha had been Tobias and Charlotte's part-time nanny for the last couple of months. As far as nannies went, she was awful, but as far as humans went, she was even worse—she was horrible, ghastly, evil, and as rotten as mayonnaise-soaked fish left out on a warm day. She yelled when it was normal to whisper, screamed when most people would just speak; she insulted everyone but their father. Recently, she had taken to shoving Charlotte around and issuing uncomfortable threats.

"I'm quite good at making things look like an accident!" Martha had told Tobias three days ago when she found dirty clothes on his bedroom floor.

Tobias had hoped she was joking, but yesterday Martha had almost pushed Charlotte down the stairs by "accident." When Tobias told his father, he only instructed Tobias to be obedient and mind his elders. But Mr. Eggers had no idea how rotten an elder Martha was. And since his dad wouldn't listen, Tobias had decided to take matters into his own hands. He looked at Martha and Charlotte as they sat at the table and cleared his throat.

"No coughing," Martha snapped. "This isn't a barn."

"Sorry," Tobias apologized. "Would you pass the gravy?"

Martha glared at him. "What?"

"The gravy." Tobias pointed.

"Would you pass the gravy, *please?*" Martha corrected snidely. "It's a delinquent who asks for things without adding *please*."

"But you said I *was* a delinquent," Tobias reminded her.

"Watch your tongue," she chastised him.

"Right," Tobias told her. "So, would you pass the gravy—*please*."

Martha pursed her thin lips and scratched at the three long hairs sticking out of her fat chin. She burped and picked up the white porcelain gravy boat.

"I'm tempted to just ignore your request," Martha said, passing the gravy. "But I've been burdened with a caring heart, and I have a difficult time being harsh."

Charlotte couldn't stop herself from laughing. She put her hand over her mouth to try and hide it.

"Excuse me," Martha snapped. "Is there something funny?"

Charlotte Eggers was exactly one year younger than her twelve-year-old brother, Tobias, but her sense of humor was just as sharp. She and Tobias shared the same birthday, March 4—the only date on the calendar that was also a command. Charlotte possessed large brown eyes that resembled dark coins in deep white wells. Her hair was shoulder length and blond, and she was constantly brushing it forward to hide her small, slightly pointed ears. For an eleven-year-old, she appeared cheerful. She looked like the kind of kid who might be used in an ad to convince others that they needed to buy something cute. In reality, she was more suited to be the spokesperson for something tricky or complicated. Charlotte was more athletic than Tobias. Alone she was fairly reasonable, but with her brother, she was good-natured, pleasantly stubborn, highly mischievous, and brutally clever. As a team, they not only attracted trouble at every turn, but if for some reason trouble didn't show up, Charlotte and Tobias would usually track it down, wait for it to fall asleep, and then stick trouble's hand in warm water so it would wet itself.

"So what is it?" Martha snapped. "What's so funny?"

"I'm just remembering a joke that Tobias told me earlier," Charlotte lied.

"Really?" Martha asked suspiciously. "Tobias told a joke? I demand to hear it."

The two children stared at her. This would be a challenge, seeing how the mood was terribly unfunny at the moment.

"On second thought," Martha said, sniffing, "don't tell me. Knowing your spirit, I'm sure the joke would be filthy."

"What?" Charlotte asked defensively.

"Save it. Your mouth's as dirty as your home."

Tobias wanted to point out that it was Martha's job to help clean up the home, but she began to eat again, and her moaning and chewing were too loud for him to get a word in edgewise. Food dripped down onto her white apron like muddy rain.

Tobias looked at his sister. It wasn't often that she was bothered, but her neck was red with frustration. He squeezed his fists and breathed out slowly. Up until now there had been a small part of him that regretted what he was going to do, but that small part had just been smothered by the way Martha was talking to Charlotte. So, with a relatively clear conscience, Tobias reached down and quietly pulled a glass jar from the front pocket of his red hoodie. He kept the jar in his lap and out of view of Martha.

Earlier that day, Tobias and Charlotte had gone on a hike. They had journeyed up to a stagnant pond located about a mile from their house. The pond was drying up and conveniently filled with tadpoles and slime. Tobias had dipped the jar into the puddle and collected hundreds of tadpoles along with a generous helping of the muck they were swimming in. He had hoped to put them in Martha's drink, but fortune had smiled, and Martha had made gravy for dinner. And Tobias believed that gravy was the perfect food to hide things in. Not only was it naturally lumpy, but it was brown.

Tobias carefully screwed the lid off the tadpole jar as he sat at the table. He popped off the top, and a whiff of putrid water drifted up under his nose and caused him to choke slightly.

Martha looked up and sniffed. It wasn't unusual for her to break wind during dinner, and she looked confused. She sniffed again, figured the smell must be hers, and then continued to go at her food.

Tobias signaled Charlotte with a nod.

"Martha?" Charlotte asked softly.

Martha stopped her gluttonous eating and stared at Charlotte. She had mashed potatoes around her lips and there was a bit of partially chewed meat dangling from one of the long strands of her poorly braided hair.

"What?" she asked, bothered. "Can't you see that I'm eating?"

"I'm sorry," Charlotte said. "I was just wondering if the time on that clock is right." Charlotte pointed to the clock hanging on the wall behind Martha. "It sounds off."

"You and your funny ears," Martha said without looking. "It's right. Clocks are always right. Now eat."

Charlotte looked at Tobias and shrugged. She had set the clock wrong earlier, hoping that Martha would turn around and look at it long enough for her brother to do what he needed. Tobias motioned for her to try again.

"So it really is ten thirty?" Charlotte asked.

Martha dropped her fork and spoon with a clang and spun around to glance at the clock. As she turned, Tobias lifted the jar of tadpoles and tilted it above the gravy bowl. The entire contents of the jar slid out in a lumpy chunk. Tobias pulled the empty jar back, and Charlotte gasped as the big wriggly blob settled into the gravy.

Martha swung around and stared at Charlotte. "Why are you gasping? So what if the clock's not set right? Have your father fix it when he gets home. Now, stop bothering me."

Tobias looked into the white gravy boat. He could see lumps squirming around in the brown sauce.

"What are you staring at?" Martha barked.

"Gravy?" Tobias offered, lifting the bowl.

"Give that here!" Martha yanked the gravy boat away from him. "What is it with you two? You have the table manners of shrews." As she scolded them, she poured a river of the altered gravy onto her potatoes and meat. Slimy brown lumps oozed around in the brown gravy, twitching and burrowing into her meal. Tobias and Charlotte saw it all, but Martha had her eyes on them. "If you were my kin, you'd be in bed right now with sore rears and empty stomachs. No wonder your mother left you."

Tobias's blue eyes burned. "She didn't leave us. She died."

"Same difference. She's gone, isn't she?" Martha picked up her spoon and fork and dug into her potatoes. While still staring Tobias down, she lifted her fork and inserted into her fat mouth one of the largest bites of gravy-covered food any human has ever taken.

Charlotte shivered as Martha's lips smacked down, sucking the wriggling gravy in.

"Stop staring," Martha commanded. She scooped up another

enormous bite and shoveled it in. "You're making it impossible for me to enjoy what I've created." As she talked, Tobias and Charlotte could see the food and the tadpoles being chomped on by Martha's crooked teeth.

Charlotte covered her eyes.

"What are you doing?" Martha scolded. "Eat."

"No thanks," Tobias said. "The gravy's a little lumpy."

Martha attempted to swallow so that she could clear her mouth and lecture Tobias. Unfortunately, the large wad of food got stuck in her throat. Her eyes flashed wide, and she glared at the Eggers children. The fat on her neck wriggled as two tadpoles slipped out of her mouth and fell onto the table. She looked at the bowl of gravy and then down at her plate at a number of squirming brown dots.

Her fat eyes bulged.

Martha pulled her hairy chin back into her neck and began to gag and spit. Her head shook as her wide tongue hung out of her mouth and her right eye twitched.

"Why, you . . . ," she sputtered angrily, reaching for her throat. "I . . . can't . . . breathe."

"You weren't supposed to take such a big bite!" Tobias said defensively. "You shoved half of your meal into your mouth."

Martha's face was growing redder as she tried to swallow what she had taken in. She banged the table with her hands as her mouth and nose leaked things that mouths and noses shouldn't leak.

"What do we do?" Charlotte asked anxiously, her brown eyes as wide as the plates they were eating from. "She wasn't supposed to choke!"

"Pat her on the back!" Tobias suggested.

Charlotte jumped up and began to slap Martha on the back. "It's not working."

"Harder!" Tobias commanded her.

Martha pounded the table, shaking frantically.

"It's not working!" Charlotte yelled. "Hug her. Do that choking thing!"

Tobias moaned and moved behind Martha. He wrapped his arms around her big body and closed his eyes. His arms barely reached around, and when he pulled back, his hands got stuck between a large doughy roll of her stomach and her bosoms. Martha shot up out of her chair, holding her throat with one hand and swinging at Tobias with the other.

"I'm trying to help!" Tobias informed her.

Martha swung and missed. Her body twisted, and she fell forward toward the two children. Charlotte pulled Tobias out of the way as Martha did a belly flop against the wood floor. The impact dislodged the food in her throat like a popped cork. A large wad of food shot out of her mouth and stuck to the wall. Then, like a balloon being untied, air raced out of Martha's lungs, ears, and behind. She coughed and sputtered, spitting gravy and tadpoles all over the kitchen. Martha caught her breath and then rolled over onto her back. She stared up at Tobias and Charlotte. The room smelled like a horrible mixture of fear and gas.

"Sorry," Tobias said lamely.

Like a messy volcano, Martha's body erupted from the floor, smoke streaming from her ears. Her brown blouse was untucked, and her apron had come untied from the back and was hanging from her neck. Martha grabbed Tobias by the collar of his red hoodie.

"How dare you?!"

"Honestly," Tobias tried. "That was a massive bite, even for you."

"You almost killed me!"

"I was about to call 9-1-1," Tobias said.

Martha's anger consumed her. She planted her feet and screamed as Tobias and Charlotte plugged their ears and leaned back on their heels.

"This was not part of my assignment," she barked. Her hair was wild, and there were traces of brown gravy and spittle foaming up around her thin lips. "This is the reason I don't have kids."

Martha stomped her feet on the floor like a spoiled child. She spun on her sensible shoes and stormed toward the front door.

"Wait," Tobias pleaded.

She kept storming.

"Seriously," Tobias hollered. "Your apron—"

Martha threw open the front door and lunged through it. As she stepped outside, an apron string caught on the edge of the door frame. The apron snagged and spun her like a top. Her body moved forward, but her neck was caught. The string ripped, and she flew down the three front steps and skidded across the lawn on her face and knees. She flopped over onto her back, giving Tobias and Charlotte a perfect view of the giant grass stain smeared across the front of her body.

Tobias ran up to her and reached down.

"No!" she screamed. "Don't touch me!"

Martha cursed as she struggled to get back up. Her large rear looked like a small brown cloud fighting to become airborne. She was still tangled in bits of apron, and there were flecks of gravy all over her. It was too much to handle; both Tobias and Charlotte began laughing.

Martha stood all the way up, shook her fists violently, tilted

her head back, and bellowed into the twilight sky like an obese wolf.

It was at that moment that something very, very bad happened—Mr. Eggers pulled into the driveway. Not that Ralph Eggers coming home was a bad thing. Normally Tobias and Charlotte were happy to see their father. No, the bad thing was that he was pulling into the driveway at the very worst possible moment. It would be quite difficult for Tobias and Charlotte to talk themselves out of something their dad could so clearly see.

It's funny how an act as normal as a father coming home early can change two children's lives forever. Not "ha-ha" funny—more like "it is the end of any happiness in our lives" funny. Which, if you think about it, really isn't that funny at all.

# CHAPTER 2

# HOW NOT TO PUNISH
# YOUR CHILDREN

Ralph Eggers had not had a particularly easy go at life. He had been born during a hurricane, gotten married during an earthquake, and lost his wife to a drowning accident. His own parents had died in a fire, his brother had been killed by a bear, and his sister had passed away in a strange country after drinking something foreign.

Ralph was a tall man with thick brown hair and small feet. He had a smooth face and no need to shave more than once a week. His eyes were brown, and they sat over his nose like two rusted pennies. He walked with a slight hunch as if he had the weight of the world on his shoulders.

Ralph struggled with holding down a job. Ever since his wife had died, it was difficult for him to focus. He had worked at seven different jobs in the last two years, and he had been fired eight times. He was fired as a mailman for dropping an important package. He was fired as a librarian for whistling too loud. He was fired as a clerk in a convenience store for insisting that a rowdy customer not "come back again." He was fired from being a waiter when he suggested the head chef should add more salt to the peas. He was fired from being a test subject in a science lab when he didn't experience any side effects from the pills he was testing. Ralph had also been fired once as a bus driver, for driving too slow, and twice as a barber—first because he refused to give a man a mullet and second because he actually did.

Life was not easy for Ralph, and things were getting worse. His two children were acting up more than ever. They had always been rather crafty kids, but lately they were acting extraordinarily spirited. Tobias constantly challenged Ralph. In the last few days alone, they had gotten into a dozen arguments over a number of dumb little things. It was as if both Tobias's and Charlotte's good-natured, pleasantly stubborn, highly mischievous, and brutally clever personalities were really exploding. And to make a bad situation even more rotten, Mr. Eggers had just been fired from being a house painter because he had mixed his primary colors all wrong.

Ralph's intentions had been to come home early and seek the solace of his children. Unfortunately, as he pulled up and saw

Martha on the lawn with a full-body grass stain and his children laughing, he lost it. The veins on his forehead throbbed, and his entire body overheated. He jumped out of the car and ran across the lawn.

Martha was screaming. "I've . . . send them away . . . Tobias!"

Tobias opened his mouth in an attempt to explain, but his father cut him off.

"Inside!" Ralph ordered his children. "Inside!"

"But . . . ," Tobias tried again.

"Now!"

Tobias and Charlotte guiltily shuffled inside as their father tried to calm Martha down.

"I'm so sorry," Ralph pleaded. "We've been having a tough time. Tobias is just going through a phase."

"Charlotte!" Martha steamed.

"Charlotte just follows his example," Ralph reasoned.

It didn't matter what Ralph Eggers said, Martha wasn't buying it. She drew in a huge breath and slapped him soundly across the cheek.

"That's for having children," Martha screamed hysterically. She slapped him again. "And that's for having *those* children."

"But—"

"Of course," Martha bellowed. "A foul word from an unfit father."

Martha picked up her ripped apron, got into her car, and drove off in a cloud of dust and gravel.

"You wanted this job!" Ralph yelled at her disappearing car.

Ralph turned slowly back to his house. The curtains quickly closed, and he could hear his children scurrying about inside. He took small, methodical steps toward the front door.

Closing his eyes, Ralph counted to ten . . . twice. He then pushed the door open and walked into the small family room. The place was eerily quiet; only the thin tick of the wrongly set clock filled the space with an uncomfortable beat. The pulsating veins on Ralph's forehead began to slow. A clear memory of his childhood flashed into his mind, giving him an idea.

"Tobias!" Mr. Eggers yelled. "Charlotte!"

Ralph heard their bedroom doors open. The sound was followed by footsteps crossing the creaky wood floor. After a few moments of silence, his children's faces appeared around the hallway corner.

"Come here," their father said.

Tobias stepped out first, and Charlotte followed. They walked toward their father and stood side by side a few feet in front of him. Standing next to each other, they looked a bit like a sad set of salt and pepper shakers. They were a pair, a set, and doubly in trouble.

"Dad, we didn't—" Tobias couldn't get his words out before his father interrupted.

"You must have holes in your head," Mr. Eggers said calmly.

While it is true that everyone has holes in his head—mouth, ears, nose, etc.—neither of the Eggers children felt it would be right to point that out to their father at the moment.

"Get in the car," Mr. Eggers ordered.

"You have to understand," Tobias tried again. "We—"

"The car!" their father insisted. "GET IN THE CAR!"

Tobias and Charlotte shuffled slowly out the door and down the steps, with their father right behind them. It was getting dark now, and the sky looked as if it was slipping into something a bit sinister.

When they got to the car, Tobias climbed into the back seat, and Charlotte got in next to him. Mr. Eggers took the driver's seat and slammed his door shut. He turned the key, and the engine roared. It was at that moment the first drops of rain began to fall. They plinked off the windows as the car wound through the neighborhood and onto the main street.

Their father drove the car onto the freeway. He pressed the gas pedal, and they flew down the interstate like a charging bull. The previously little raindrops became gushy wads of water that slapped at the windshield as they raced on.

Mr. Eggers kept his hands on the steering wheel in the positions of ten and two o'clock. His knuckles were white, and the back of his neck looked like a steamed ham. He stared straight ahead through the wet windshield and out at the dark road. The rain grew stronger, and the car shivered as the wild wind blew through it.

"He looks pretty mad," Charlotte whispered to Tobias.

"That's a look worse than mad," Tobias said.

Headlights from the cars on the other side of the freeway flashed past them. In the rain the lights appeared messy and shot past them like wet sneezes. Mr. Eggers kept his eyes on the road and drove directly into the storm.

"My stomach hurts," Charlotte said.

"Mine too," Tobias agreed. "I really didn't think Martha would take such a big bite."

A sad and silent half an hour later, their father turned on his blinker and they exited the freeway. The rain seemed to slow as they traveled east down a small two-lane highway. Tobias and Charlotte gazed out the dark windows. There were no lights anywhere. It was just a dark, wet desert with little form or definition.

"It looks like there's nothing out here," Charlotte whimpered.

As if on cue, a large weathered sign came into view: WITHERWOOD.

Just past the sign, Ralph Eggers turned off the highway onto a small road. The road was straight for a few hundred feet and then grew twisty and steep. Tobias and Charlotte rocked back and forth as the car turned and climbed up the road to the top of the dark mesa.

"I'm going to be sick," Charlotte grunted.

The road leveled out, and Mr. Eggers brought the vehicle to a stop. Through the windshield, Tobias saw the headlights shining on what looked like the bars of a large gate. Their father turned around and stared at them.

"Get out," he said calmly.

"What?" Tobias asked nervously. "Here?"

"Maybe Martha was right," their father said. "If you choose to act like brats, then maybe it's time somebody else raised you."

"Dad," Charlotte said, shocked. "Martha's awful."

"Out," Mr. Eggers repeated.

"You can't just leave us here," Tobias said angrily. "It's nighttime, and we're in the middle of nowhere!"

"You made this decision," Mr. Eggers said, determined to stay tough. "Everything's a joke to you. Well, no more. Now out."

Tobias pushed open the door and stepped into the dark night. He stumbled a little as he turned to look back into the car. "Come on, Char."

"We can't just stay here," Charlotte argued. "Dad!"

Mr. Eggers turned and stared out the windshield.

"Out," he said one last time.

Charlotte took Tobias's hand and climbed out of the car. It wasn't raining at the moment, but the air was moist and it mixed with the tears on her cheeks, making her feel wet all over. Their car moved in reverse and then spun to the side and turned around. They watched in horror as the rear lights grew smaller and smaller. They stood there on the side of the road in disbelief.

"He'll be back," Tobias said, trying to comfort his sister. "He's just trying to scare us."

"Well, it's working."

Tobias kept his arm around Charlotte as she stared into the distance, willing her father's car lights to reappear. A gentle rain started falling, and their wet hair and clothes made their bodies feel as heavy as their hearts.

"Where are we, anyway?" Charlotte asked, sniffling.

"We're on the top of some hill," Tobias guessed.

"What was that gate?"

They had been so intent on staring down the road that neither of them had turned to look in the other direction. As they twisted their heads, a weak lamp high atop a wooden pole buzzed. It shone for a second and then went dark again.

"Did you see that?" Charlotte asked.

"It was kinda hard to miss," Tobias replied.

The light sparked on once more, and they saw a massive brick wall with an iron gate between two huge stone pillars.

Charlotte squeezed Tobias's right hand. "What is that place?"

"I don't know," Tobias said. "Looks like something from a book or movie."

"It's no chocolate factory," Charlotte whispered.

Tobias took a deep breath. "Yeah, it doesn't smell like chocolate."

The light snapped off, and once again darkness smothered them. They both turned their heads to look in the direction of the winding road.

"I hope Dad comes to his senses soon," Charlotte said, shivering.

"Me too," Tobias replied. "Me too."

It's sad how sometimes you can hope all you want, but still the thing you hope for is just not going to happen. Very sad indeed.

# CHAPTER 3

# SLICK ROADS AND HIDDEN RIVERS

Ralph Eggers drove slowly down the steep, twisting road. Most level-headed people might think Ralph was out of his mind, and they would be right. Ralph, however, believed he was doing something good. You see, years ago, when Ralph was a kid, he had accidentally set his tree house on fire while playing with matches. So Ralph's father, in an effort to teach him a lesson, had driven him out to the same spot and dropped him off. Ralph's dad thought he needed to be shocked into understanding. It had worked for Ralph. He cried for twenty minutes, and then his father had driven back up the mesa and picked him up. Since that day, Ralph had never lit anything on fire. Even now he still had a hard time using a gas stove or lighting a water heater.

Ralph reached the bottom of the mesa and turned onto the two-lane road. After a couple of miles, he exited the road and stopped near an abandoned rest area. He shut off the car and listened to the tiny raindrops hitting the top of the roof. He knew his children would be terrified, but he was hoping the terror would teach them a powerful lesson.

"This is for the best," he said, trying hard to convince himself.

It didn't work. His shoulders began to shake, and his body bounced up and down as he cried softly. He wiped at his eyes and tried to catch his breath.

"I am quite possibly the worst dad ever."

The situation he had found when he came home was awful, but it now felt far less drastic than what he had just done. He had loathed his father when he had done this horrible thing, and now he had done the same to the only two people who mattered to him in the world.

Ralph wanted to mourn the loss of his wife. He also wanted to scream about his troubled life and the situation he was in. But more than anything, he wanted to get back to his children. The anger he felt had subsided, and in its wake was a searing guilt.

"I've done a foolish thing."

He started his car and drove to the edge of the road.

"I'm coming!" he hollered.

Ralph gunned it and flew along the road at eighty miles an hour.

"What was I thinking?" he said, chastising himself.

Half a mile before the Witherwood sign, a large animal jumped out of the darkness and ran directly in front of Ralph's car. He turned the wheel, missing the creature and driving off the highway. The car raced down a steep ravine, crashing through cedar trees. It slammed into a large boulder, flipped twice, and came to a stop upside down at the bottom of the tree-covered ravine. The wheels spun as the car settled, and the headlights flashed twice before darkening.

Ralph Eggers was going to be a little late picking up his children.

# CHAPTER 4

# THE IRON GATE

The Eggers children stood in the dark like two shadows. Tobias lifted his chin and looked up into the wet black sky. It should be noted that while Tobias possessed clear blue eyes, it was the swatch of freckles that ran beneath them that made him striking. Depending on his mood and the lighting, Tobias's freckles always looked a little different.

"How could he do this?" Tobias growled, his freckles wet and dark.

"We shouldn't have done that to Martha," Charlotte said.

"Dad doesn't even know what we did," Tobias said. "Maybe Martha was attacking us."

"Dad's not stupid."

"Still," Tobias insisted. "That doesn't mean he can just dump us at night in the middle of nowhere."

The rain began to pick up.

"While it's raining," Tobias added.

"He's been really sad lately," Charlotte reminded Tobias.

"Well, he's not the only one," Tobias said. "I still miss Mom."

Charlotte didn't like thinking about the mother she had lost three years ago. The green T-shirt she was wearing ironically had the word HOPE printed across the front of it. Well, hope seemed to be absent as water trickled down her arms and pooled in her shoes.

"Mom never would have done this," Tobias said.

"I'm cold," Charlotte whispered.

"So am I, and I'm not waiting here any longer. If Dad thinks I won't go in there, then he's wrong." Tobias pointed to the foreboding iron gate. "He dropped us here, so we should go in. Maybe it's nice inside."

The light on top of the pole buzzed on, again exposing the gate. The bulb flickered three times and then snapped off.

Charlotte shivered. "It doesn't look very nice. Let's just wait here."

"No way," Tobias insisted.

"Let's walk back down to the highway," Charlotte suggested. "Dad might be there waiting."

"That's probably what he wants," Tobias said strongly.

Charlotte followed her big brother. The outlines of the bars were slightly visible against the black clouds. As they stepped closer, the bars grew taller and taller, the tops of them piercing the sky like knives.

They reached the gate, and the broken light buzzed on and kept its glow for a few seconds. The edges of the gate were covered in thorny vines, and there were words etched into the stone pillars on the side of the bars. Tobias pulled at the back of his hair as he read aloud, "Witherwood Reform School—Caring, Community, and Character since 1805."

"Sounds cheery," Charlotte observed. "Do you think they didn't care before 1805?"

Tobias tried to laugh.

The light buzzed off. Tobias stepped up to the gate and grabbed two of the thick bars. They were wet and cold and felt imposing in his hands. He shoved hard, but the gate wouldn't move. He inhaled deeply.

The death of his mom had affected Tobias in a strange way. Ever since she had died, things in life smelled and tasted different and much stronger.

"How's it smell?" Charlotte asked.

"Dark," Tobias replied.

"It looks pretty shut up," Charlotte observed. "Maybe there's no one in there."

Tobias pushed his face against the bars and stared with his

wet blue eyes. Through the dark he saw a cobblestone road, and in the distance, he spotted two little lights on a high wall.

"Look," he whispered excitedly.

Charlotte pushed her face up to the bars and gazed fervently. "I don't see anything."

"Way, way back there," Tobias insisted. "It's the top of a building. And look, there are some small rocks glowing on the ground."

Charlotte could see small iridescent stones twinkling softly, like dim stars stuck to the ground; the building was too dark to make out. She turned and looked back down the road, wishing her father would return.

"He's not there," Tobias said, realizing what she was doing. "We'll go inside, and when Dad comes back, we'll tell him we're not sure we want to go yet."

The thought was so ridiculous it caused Charlotte to smile.

"Yeah," she said. "We can tell him we need to check our calendars."

"See?" Tobias laughed. "We can do this."

"But we can't even get in," Charlotte reminded him. "Unless you think you can pick that lock."

Before Tobias could answer, a buzzing noise came from the gate. It was followed by a sharp click.

"I think we were just buzzed in," Tobias said nervously.

"Is that good or bad?" Charlotte whispered.

"I have no idea. I guess somebody can see us on a camera or something."

Charlotte waved at the darkness just in case someone was watching. While she waved, Tobias put both hands on the bars and pushed as hard as he could. The iron gate squealed like a pig. He moved it open three feet and then stood back and stared at the opening.

"Maybe we should wait here," Charlotte said again.

"It's just a school," Tobias reminded her. "How bad can it be?"

It was a foolish question. Certainly there are some fantastic schools in the world, places of great learning, fulfillment, and excitement. But none of the schools Tobias and Charlotte had ever been to had been that kind of school.

"Right," Tobias corrected himself. "I mean, it's probably no worse than our school now. Besides, their motto is 'Caring, Community, and Character,' remember?"

"Building character is so painful sometimes," Charlotte said.

"Well, do you want to stand out here in the rain all night?"

Charlotte shook her head.

Tobias slipped through the opening and back behind the bars. He then reached out his hand. "Come on, Char."

Charlotte extended her arm and took Tobias's hand.

"You shouldn't have put those tadpoles in Martha's gravy."

"Enough with that. She shouldn't have pushed you around. Besides, it's too late to worry about that now."

"Yup," Charlotte agreed. "I think we have new things to worry about."

The gate light flickered twice as a soft wind picked up.

# CHAPTER 5

# ONE-MAN WELCOME PARTY

*There are times in life when a person knows he or she is doing wrong, but for some odd reason, continues doing it. A woman might realize she's going the wrong way, but she keeps going because she's too proud to stop and ask for directions. A man might discover that what he's cooking is horrible, but he keeps cooking it because he believes the woman who won't stop to ask for directions will be over any moment and she'll expect something to eat. In the end they're both going to be disappointed and realize that they should have stopped before they began. Well, it would have been wise for Tobias to stop before he began, but being a bit stubborn, he led Charlotte toward the school.*

**T**his place is creepy," Charlotte whispered. "I don't care for the trees. They look as if they're going to attack us."

The trees she was concerned about were tall cottonwoods and willows that lined the cobblestone road. In the dark, their leafy branches reached out like strands of webbing waiting to ensnare them.

"I promise the trees won't attack us," Tobias assured her.

"We should probably turn back," Charlotte said, having a bad case of second and third thoughts. "Dad's going to be looking for us."

"Don't worry," Tobias insisted. "When Dad returns and finds we're gone, he'll be so sick about it that he'll beg to be forgiven. I figure us coming in here will erase any punishment those tadpoles might have caused."

The cobblestone road was outlined faintly by tiny white pebbles. They followed the road as it turned to the right and then curved to the left. When it straightened out, the dark silhouette of a large three-story building began to appear. The night made it hard to see clearly, but there were at least fifty unlit, arched windows, and bulky square stones framed the far corners. Ivy clung to the bottom of the building like leafy fingers. Witherwood looked a bit like a flattened castle that had forgotten to be enchanted.

Both Tobias and Charlotte stopped and took a moment to stare.

"That doesn't look like a school," Charlotte whispered. "It's huge."

They followed the cobblestone road up to a circular drive that wrapped around a good-sized statue of a man . . . or a woman. It was hard to tell for sure because it was so old and weathered. Behind the statue, a path led to the ivy-covered front. Over the doors hung a large copper overhang. A weak yellow light lit up the wide double doors.

Tobias and Charlotte took the path and then stood under the copper overhang trying to find the courage to enter.

"Can you hear someone singing?" Charlotte asked.

"No. Who would be singing here?"

Above the doors, the word WITHERWOOD was chiseled in stone. The doors themselves were wooden, with smiling eagles carved on the bottom panels. The happy eagles had sticks in their mouths and flags in their talons. Just above the eagles were giant wooden knockers shaped like round moons. Carved at the top of both doors were the words EDUCATION, EDUCATION, EDUCATION. It may have been the wind, but it sounded like the huge school was moaning softly.

Tobias reached out and grabbed the knob on the left door. He tried to twist the knob, but it wouldn't budge. He tried the other; it was locked as well. Tobias looked at Charlotte and squeezed a handful of wet hair on the back of his head.

"Maybe nobody goes to school here anymore," Charlotte suggested. "It's really quiet."

Tobias grabbed one of the knockers. He lifted it and let it fall. A loud, dull bonk echoed from behind the door.

"Did you hear that?" Charlotte asked.

"No."

"I can hear someone coming!"

Tobias's heart began to thump wildly. The hairs on the back of his neck stretched as if trying to scream.

The noise grew louder.

*Pllumpt. Pllumpt.*

"That doesn't sound normal," Charlotte insisted.

"It's fine," Tobias said, attempting to act casual. "It's just foot-steps. Someone must be coming."

*Pllumpt. Pllumpt.*

"I smell something old," Tobias said quietly.

The footsteps ceased, but they were followed by the clank and scrape of what sounded like chains being moved, and then a key being turned and a lock tumbling open.

*Click.*

The left door opened slowly. Tobias and Charlotte held their breath, staring at the widening gap. There it was, the source of the old smell. Through the opening, they saw an extremely short man wearing a white overcoat and peering at them with his left eye. Tobias glanced down. On his small feet, the man had black shoes that were in need of a good polishing. Charlotte looked at the top of him and discovered he was bald and sporting a gray comb-over with no more than four long hairs. The man also had a pointed chin and a nose that was caught between trying to decide whether it should turn up or turn down—one nostril was visible, and the other was not. He looked funny, but not in a good way.

"Hello?" the short man said nervously, scratching his right forearm.

"Hello," Tobias said back.

"We're closed for the day," the man informed them.

"I know," Tobias said. "It's just that—"

"It's late," the little man interrupted. "Very late. Most people are asleep at this time."

"Right," Tobias said. "We're really sorry about that. It's just that we were stranded outside your gate and wondered if we could wait here until our father comes back."

"Stranded?" the funny little man asked, acting more frightened than they were. "My goodness. Did one of the . . . did someone bring you here?"

"We were dropped off," Charlotte explained. "Our dad—"

Tobias elbowed Charlotte to shut her up. "What my sister means is that our father dropped us off by accident."

"Accident?" the little man asked, opening the door a bit more. "This is a school, not an accident. Our motto is—"

"Sure," Tobias interrupted. "We saw the sign. We just need someplace to wait for our dad. Or maybe you have a phone we could use?" It was a silly thing to ask for, since there wasn't a single person besides his father who Tobias could call for help, and Tobias knew his father didn't have a phone.

"I'm curious," the little man asked. "How'd you get through the gate?"

"Someone buzzed it open," Tobias explained. "Was it you?"

"No, but that's interesting. And you're sure you're not here to harm our school?"

Tobias looked down at his sister and then back at the man. "We're sure."

The large wood door closed just a bit and then, with one creaking motion, it swung all the way open.

"Come in," the man said smoothly. "I'd kick myself in the morning if I didn't lend a helping hand. And who wants to be kicked?"

"Not us," Tobias and Charlotte answered in unison.

The little man smiled and waved them in.

This was the third time in the last few hours they had felt things were wrong but just kept on going. They stepped inside Witherwood, and the wood door shut behind them with a piercing snap.

# CHAPTER 6

# THERE'S SOMETHING IN THE TREES

Inside Witherwood, the darkness of the great outdoors was gone, thanks to long fluorescent lights overhead that flickered slightly. The funny little man limped over to a desk and motioned for them to sit down. Two empty chairs were positioned in the middle of the floor, looking almost as if they had been set up for the children's arrival.

"It's like you knew we were coming," Tobias joked.

"We didn't," the man replied quickly. "I am told a lot of things, but I didn't know about you two. Please sit down."

Tobias and Charlotte sat. They were dripping wet and appeared smaller than normal. Charlotte glanced around, taking in her surroundings. The room was big and rectangular. The bottom half of the walls was painted blue, and the top was white. The ceiling was made of a brown glossy wood that matched the doors and the trim. There was a poster on one wall of a giraffe attempting to swallow a watermelon. The caption below it read, *Some things aren't worth trying.*

"That's weird," Charlotte whispered.

Next to the giraffe poster was a map of Witherwood. Tobias stared at it. He had been interested in maps since he was a little kid. He loved the makeup of buildings and the mechanics of machines. The map of Witherwood showed that the school was rectangular, with a massive open space in the middle. The four sides of the school were labeled—East Hall, where they now were; Severe Hall, which was the south part of the school; Never Hall, the north; and Weary Hall, the back of the school. There were other buildings and structures drawn on the map, but they were blocked by a tall lamp and hard to see. Overall, the map wasn't as detailed as Tobias would have liked.

"Not a very good map," Tobias whispered to his sister.

"I knew you'd say that," she whispered back.

The room had a large glass trophy case that ran the length of the back wall. There were only five trophies in the case. The floor was white marble with gray specks and had a number of cracks in it. An empty fish tank was pushed up against one of the walls. It was sloppily filled with books and papers. Taped to the front of the fish tank was a single piece of white paper with STUDENT MORALE DAY IS COMING written on it. The room seemed more functional than interesting.

The little man sat down behind a large wood desk and opened the top drawer. While rummaging through it, he spoke. "My name is Orrin. You can call me Mr. Orrin if you need to, but most people think it's easier to just say Orrin. It's my last name. My first name, quite frankly, is none of your business—not to be rude, just honest."

Tobias wanted to point out that they didn't need to know his name or anything about him, since they wouldn't be there very long.

"I'm one of the . . . teachers," Orrin continued. "Curious story about that. I entered a contest in a magazine called *Hard to Explain*. The winner got to be a science teacher for a day here at Witherwood. I won, and well, after that day I just couldn't leave. I've been here for years. And it just so happens that it's my turn to watch the front tonight. We take turns around here. We're like a big family."

Both kids nodded and noticed that Orrin's eyes didn't match. One was light blue, while the other looked almost black. He also had a red rash on his right forearm that he kept scratching.

Orrin found what he was looking for in his drawer. "Aha, just what I needed," he said, pulling out a small white index card. He slipped a pen from his coat pocket and clicked the top of it. "Your names, please?"

"I'm Tobias, and my sister's name is Charlotte."

Orrin wrote the names down and then looked up. "Your surname?"

Tobias was confused. "Um . . . I'm Sir Tobias?"

"No, no," Orrin said, trying not to smile. "Your last name?"

"Oh, why do you need that? We won't be here for long. Our dad's probably coming through the gate right now."

"The gate's locked," Orrin said. "It's important to keep things where they belong."

"But we left it open," Tobias told him.

"Interesting. Well, if you don't want to give me your last name, so be it." He put the small white card into a box on his desk that was filled with other small white cards organized alphabetically. "I'd let you use the phone, but this wet weather ruins our phone lines up here on the mesa. Can't make a single call."

"Oh," Tobias said, staring at the little box Orrin had put the card in.

"It wouldn't help anyhow. Our dad doesn't have a cell phone," Charlotte said. "And we haven't got anyone else to—"

Tobias elbowed Charlotte, and she shut up.

"Interesting," Orrin said again. "Well, then maybe you'd like to lie down? I'm sure we could find a spot for you to rest. I find rest to be most comforting."

"That's okay," Tobias said. "We'll just rest in these chairs."

"Fine," Orrin replied, leaning back in his own chair and closing his mismatched eyes.

"You don't have to stay with us," Tobias said. "I promise we won't touch anything."

Orrin opened his eyes and smiled—a small dimple appeared on his left cheek. "It's not the school I'm worried about."

Tobias suddenly wished he were standing outside in the dark getting rained on instead of being inside with Orrin. "You know, maybe we should just go."

"Yeah," Charlotte agreed, her face pale.

"The gate's locked," Orrin said, scratching at his arm.

"I'll go check," Tobias told him. "I'm pretty sure we left it open."

"It's locked now. Trust me," Orrin insisted. "I think it'd be best if you just stayed right here until your father comes. Okay?"

Tobias and Charlotte looked at him and nodded.

"You've actually arrived at a great time. Student Morale Day is not that far away and—"

Orrin's words were cut off by a muffled scream that was coming from someplace in the school. Tobias and Charlotte jumped out of their chairs. Orrin barely flinched.

"What was that?" Tobias asked.

"Don't worry about that. This is such an old building. There are lots of odd noises. It's probably just someone flushing a toilet, or maybe it's the foundation settling."

"Are you kidding? That wasn't settling," Tobias said. "We need to go."

"The gate's locked," Orrin reminded them. "Please, stay seated."

"No, really," Tobias said, grabbing Charlotte's hand. "We've got to go."

"I wouldn't if I were you," Orrin warned. "I'm only trying to help. That's my job, helping students."

The sound of someone singing down the hall drifted into the room; large goose bumps ran up the Eggers kids' backs. Both of them stood.

"Do your toilets sing too?" Tobias said worriedly.

"Please just sit, and I'll explain," Orrin started.

Tobias bolted for the door, yanking Charlotte behind him. He pulled the door open and charged out. It was still raining, but the open door lit up the cobblestone drive.

"Come on!" Tobias yelled.

"I'm coming!" Charlotte yelled back. "It's not like I want to stop and look at things."

Their feet slapped across the wet cobblestones as they ran past the weathered statue and back toward the gate. It was dark, yet the small glowing rocks showed them the outline of the road. There was no sound of Orrin giving chase.

"There's the gate light," Charlotte said, pointing straight ahead. "Keep going!"

In the distance, the broken light flickered. They both sprinted. Charlotte was the first to reach the gate. She grabbed two of the large bars and pulled. Three seconds later, Tobias was right beside her, pulling on some bars of his own.

"Someone really did lock it," Tobias complained, looking around frantically.

"What was that scream in there?" Charlotte asked. "That was no toilet."

"I know," Tobias answered. "And did you see where he filed our card?"

"No."

"Under *E*," Tobias answered. "We didn't tell him our last name. How would he know it starts with *E*?"

"Maybe Dad told him," Charlotte said, confused. "Maybe he really did mean to leave us here. Maybe this is part of the lesson he's trying to teach us. Or maybe it's just a coincidence."

"Whatever it is, I'm not staying."

"Can you open the lock?" Charlotte asked.

"Not without some tools. Here, get on my shoulders."

"What'll that do?"

"Maybe you'll be tall enough to hop over the gate."

"Then what?"

"I don't know," Tobias said loudly. "Climb down the other side, I guess. At least you'll be out. Then when Dad gets back, you can point at me trapped in here and make fun of me for being such an idiot."

"As great as that sounds, even on your shoulders, I still wouldn't be tall enough to get over this gate. And knowing you, I'd probably get dropped."

"Fine," Tobias said, bothered. "What if we just did what we did when they buzzed us in?"

"We didn't do anything," Charlotte reminded him.

"Maybe it was our talking." Tobias stared at the bars and in his friendliest voice said, "We'd like to leave now."

The gate remained locked, and Charlotte could hear a low growling filling the air behind them. She jumped on Tobias and tried to pull herself up on top of him.

"What are you doing?"

"I'm taking your suggestion."

Tobias helped Charlotte onto his shoulders, and she stood up, holding the bars for balance. Even standing with her right arm outstretched, she was still a good three feet away from the top of the gate.

The growling behind them turned into a roar.

Tobias wobbled, and Charlotte came crashing down. Her right

knee slammed into his face as she rolled off him and onto the cobblestones. There was no time to lick their wounds.

Tobias jumped up. "Get to the trees!"

The sound of large, heavy feet slapping down against the cobblestone road was growing louder and quicker.

"Hurry!" Tobias yelled.

"I'm more worried about you," Charlotte hollered as she passed him.

Looking back, Tobias could see two huge eyes charging toward them. His heart raced faster than his legs as his eyes searched for help in the darkness.

"Over here!" Charlotte yelled. "There's a low branch!"

Another terrifying roar ripped through the air.

Tobias reached the low branch and jumped up onto it. Charlotte grabbed a limb above him. Tobias pushed her from below as she pulled herself higher.

"Climb as high as you can!" he hollered.

Tobias jumped from the branch he was on as a large paw swiped at him. The limb cracked and tore. He was now hanging from the higher branch with his legs kicking in the air, frantically pulling himself up as the animal beneath him roared. The creature swiped again. The tip of its claw caught the heel of Tobias's sneaker and tore off a chunk of rubber.

"Hurry!" Tobias yelled. "Climb!"

Charlotte was already two branches above him and moving even higher. Tobias jumped to the next limb, his hands and elbows scraping and tearing against the bark as he did his best imitation of a frantic monkey.

The animal clawed at the tree, but it was obvious that it was having a difficult time getting any higher. Charlotte reached the top branches and crawled in close to the trunk. She wrapped one arm around the tree and reached out for Tobias with the other. Tobias moved up and sat on a thick branch next to his sister. The two of them held on to each other and listened to the animal. Again and again, the beast could be heard trying to climb and then falling back down to the ground. After a few minutes, it sniffed loudly and stomped off. It was another five minutes before Tobias's and Charlotte's breathing had calmed enough for them to speak.

"What was that?" Charlotte finally asked.

"I don't know. I thought we were dead."

"I thought we were food," Charlotte said seriously. "What do we do now?"

Tobias looked down into the dark. He glanced around at the leaves they were hidden under. His hands hurt, and his legs were still burning from the climb.

"I guess we wait up here for Dad."

In the distance, they heard dogs barking. The noise grew louder and then faded completely, until there was nothing but the plinking of rain against the leaves. Looking down, they could see hundreds of tiny stones glowing softly and making them feel as if they were gazing into space.

"Do you think someone will come to help us?" Charlotte whispered.

"Of course," Tobias said.

Charlotte became silent as Tobias sat there wondering why tadpoles didn't come with warning labels.

# CHAPTER 7

# THE MOURNING MORNING

*Some people like to camp. There are also people who enjoy swallowing swords and eating Brussels sprouts. The world is full of kooks. I suppose the version of camping where you stay in a nice hotel with a pool and a free hot breakfast might be bearable. But that wasn't the case for Tobias and Charlotte. They were camping in the top of a tree, near a strange school, with frightening animals lurking below them. As the sun finally began to rise and their night of impromptu camping came to an end, their view of the world began to change.*

What was once darkness below was now a desert floor filled with beautiful flowers and unusual foliage. The top of the mesa was crammed with large, aging cottonwoods that stood like withered soldiers on a tall tower. The tree Tobias and Charlotte were in swayed and creaked under the influence of a light wind. The children had taken turns sleeping, but neither one could relax for fear of falling. Through a break in the branches, they could see the top of the iron gate. The air smelled wet, but the morning sky was yellow and warm.

Tobias's blue eyes scanned the horizon. His freckles were faint and almost invisible.

The two were frightened, but daylight and the sound of birds chirping turned the top of the mesa into something far less foreboding and almost welcoming.

"I know life's been kinda strange lately," Charlotte said. "But I didn't think I'd be waking up in a tree."

"Yeah, but we're okay, and I know Dad will come through that gate and take us away."

"Really?" Charlotte asked skeptically.

"Well, it's not like they can keep us here," Tobias said defensively. "Dad might have acted crazy last night, but he'll be back. He has to."

Two large red birds with long tails flew overhead, smearing the mustard-colored sky like streaks of feathery ketchup. The birds screamed and circled back.

"This place is weird," Tobias said, looking out through the branches toward the noisy fowl.

"I know," Charlotte said. "And what was that thing last night?"

"Orrin?" Tobias joked. "Aw, he's just short and trying to hide the fact that he's bald."

"Not Orrin. The thing that tore up your shoe."

"I couldn't see well in the dark. It had huge eyes and smelled like wet carpet."

The sound of dogs barking in the distance interrupted him. They both sat up tall in the tree and listened carefully.

"Maybe they're looking for us?" Tobias said hopefully.

"Over here!" Charlotte shouted.

The barking grew louder, and they continued to scream and holler until a pack of dogs were directly beneath them and barking as if they'd treed a couple of coons. Holding on to the dogs was Orrin. Behind Orrin were a few men in long yellow lab coats. Orrin held his left hand above his two-colored eyes and looked up. From where Tobias and Charlotte were sitting, he didn't look much taller than the dogs. The hounds began to howl.

"Quiet, please," Orrin ordered the dogs. "No need for all the noise now!"

One by one, the dogs stopped their barking and reluctantly lay down.

"Is that them?" one of the men in yellow asked Orrin.

"Of course that's them," Orrin replied. "What do you think,

we just have kids scattered around in the tops of trees? Times aren't like they used to be. Are you two okay?" Orrin yelled up.

"Fine," Tobias hollered down. "I lost part of my shoe."

"You're fortunate you didn't lose more than that," Orrin said in a nice sort of way. "It was dark last night."

"And there was some weird animal out here," Tobias hollered. "We couldn't tell what it was."

"Like I said, it was dark. You should have never left the office. Can you climb down?"

"I think so," Tobias said.

Charlotte tugged on Tobias's red hoodie. "Wait, are you sure we should? I mean, we were sort of running from him."

Tobias looked down at Orrin and the dogs while Orrin looked up.

"Your father's going to be relieved," Orrin yelled.

"What?" Charlotte asked. A tiny tinge of hope was beginning to rise from her toes and up through her body.

"Your father," Orrin yelled. "He's here. He's on the other side of the mesa looking for you. You've got him worried sick. Poor man."

That was all the encouragement the Eggers kids needed. Tobias jumped down to the branch beneath him, with Charlotte right behind.

"I told you," Tobias said as they both started climbing down the tree. "Now, don't act too happy. We want Dad to pay for this."

"Right," Charlotte agreed.

They both descended to the next branch.

"Man, Dad's gonna owe us," Tobias said.

"Carefully," Orrin hollered. "Your father would never forgive me if you got hurt climbing down."

After a few more swings and one good shimmy, the Eggers kids dropped to the ground right next to the dogs and a couple of broken branches.

"There we go." Orrin smiled. "You two are pretty brave. I've never been able to climb trees. I have the knees of an old man. Now, come on."

Tobias and Charlotte followed Orrin closely as the men in yellow walked behind them.

"When did our dad come?" Tobias asked.

"It was very late," Orrin answered. "We tried to find you, but like I said, it was dark. No matter now. All's good that ends good."

Orrin stopped walking and handed the dogs' leashes to the other two men. They took the hounds and walked off in a different direction. Orrin motioned for Charlotte and Tobias to follow him.

"Do you know what that thing chasing us last night was?" Tobias asked.

Orrin cleared his throat—it was not a pleasant sound. He sniffed twice and said, "It was probably just a stray dog."

"It wasn't a dog," Charlotte insisted.

"Sometimes things look different in the night," Orrin said condescendingly. "One time I thought I saw a person hiding outside my window. It turned out to be a bush. I wasted all that worrying for a bush. Silly me."

Charlotte looked at Orrin as if he were crazy.

"So maybe what you saw last night was a bush or a loose bag blowing in the wind. Now, come along."

In no time, they were back on the cobblestone road and walking toward the front of the school. Everything appeared older and more majestic in the daylight. The worn red rocks that made up the cobblestone road were smooth and uneven, and looked like they'd been placed there when the earth was formed. There was also a sort of sparkle to the school, making it look much more enchanting than it did at night.

"Are we on top of a hill?" Tobias asked.

"This is no hill," Orrin said proudly. "This is a mesa, which is the Spanish word for 'table.'"

"It feels so high," Charlotte said.

"It's quite high and quite spectacular. You should feel lucky to be here."

They reached the statue at the front of the school, and Orrin stopped. The weathered statue was a bit easier to make out in the daylight. It was shaped like a man with books under his left arm. His right hand was broken off. At his feet were three stone creatures that may or may not have been frogs. The whole thing was worn, and there were thorny weeds growing from the statue's ears, nose, and backside. A thin trickle of water was dripping from the statue's mouth, making the man look a bit like a drooling idiot.

"We'll have you wait inside while the orderlies fetch your father," Orrin said.

The children followed Orrin to the double front doors under the copper overhang and into the office. The two wood chairs they had sat in the night before were now pushed up against the wall. Orrin closed the doors and locked them. The noise of his key turning and the lock snapping seemed to awaken something in both Tobias and Charlotte.

"Wait," Tobias asked. "Where'd you say my dad was?"

"On the other side of the mesa. Behind the school. Now, please have a seat."

Tobias and Charlotte sat in the chairs.

"So our dad finally came late last night?" Charlotte asked.

Orrin nodded and smiled. "It was such a relief for him to show up."

"What time?" she added.

"I'm not sure," Orrin replied. "I don't wear a watch."

"I didn't hear any cars," Charlotte said.

"Perhaps you weren't listening. Sometimes children don't listen."

"She has really good ears," Tobias defended his sister.

"They do look unusual."

Tobias looked at Orrin and then back at Charlotte. His sister's brown eyes were black, and the smile she occasionally sported was upside down and stiff at the corners. It was really a frown. Her ears twitched as if she were a fox on alert.

Tobias ignored Orrin's comment and said, "I bet our dad's beard looked funny all wet."

"Sure," Orrin replied. "I guess it did. Ha ha. What fun. I never could grow a beard."

Tobias stood—Charlotte copied him perfectly. They both began to back toward the door.

"What's gotten into you kids?" Orrin asked. "Please sit down."

"Our dad doesn't have a beard," Tobias shot back.

Orrin stared at them as his smile faded into a frown. "Oh, I see. Well, how would I know if he did or he didn't? I've never met him."

"You said he's here," Charlotte reminded him.

"I guess I lied," Orrin replied. "I shouldn't have, but I did.

And now, since that's cleared up, why don't you please sit down and we'll continue where we left off last night."

Orrin took the same small white card out of the tiny box and pulled a pen from his coat pocket.

"Be reasonable and sit down," he suggested. "Standing will make you tired. Besides, the door's locked and there's nowhere to run."

"This isn't right," Charlotte insisted.

"I don't think he cares," Tobias said.

Orrin sniffed and then sat up straight. "I do care. But let's be reasonable. Your father brought you here. You said yourself that you were 'dropped off.' "

"It was a mistake," Tobias said angrily. "It has to be."

"Mistake or not, you're here now, and he's nowhere to be found. Sometimes you play the hand you're dealt."

Charlotte stared at Orrin. "Our father wouldn't leave us."

"It appears that he did," Orrin said sadly.

The words were painful to hear. No kids want to know that those who are supposed to care for them no longer do. Besides, bad news like that is best delivered by a note or a friend. Tobias and Charlotte were getting the news from a short bald man with bad breath and hair in his ears. The reality of what was happening made it hard for them to even hold their heads up.

"Have a seat," Orrin said, scratching his arm harder.

Tobias lifted his eyes and looked around. They were trapped. He shuffled back to his chair and sat down. It took Charlotte a few minutes to comply, but eventually she took her seat right next to her brother.

"Much better," Orrin said, clicking his pen. "So much better. Now, where were we? Oh yes, you ran off before I was able to formally greet you. Welcome to Witherwood, where caring, community, and character are as important as education. I trust your stay will be rewarding."

Tobias and Charlotte shivered.

"Excellent," Orrin said proudly. "As I said before, you've come at a great time. The Student Morale parade is only a week away. It's a gift the teachers give the students. Children line the path in the gardens, and they get to wave at the floats to their heart's content. Such a special occasion, like Wither Week, or Saint Trimmings Day. Look at me babble. Let's start where we should. How 'bout you tell me your last name."

"I think you already know that," Tobias said dejectedly.

"I believe you're right."

Orrin smiled and all hope exited the room. They watched him write something on the small white card.

"I don't understand," Charlotte said. "How could you possibly know our names?"

"Well," Orrin said proudly, "we like to keep track of certain children. And I suppose you stand out. After all, it's not often we get a set."

Tobias and Charlotte shivered in a way that made all their previous shivering seem weak, outdated, and completely lacking.

"Welcome to Witherwood, Tobias and Charlotte Eggers," Orrin said properly. "I trust your stay will be . . . well, let's just say, I trust you'll stay."

# CHAPTER 8

## THE GARDENS
## OF WITHERWOOD

*The world is divided into parts. There are parts most people like, comfortable, fun, exciting parts. There are bits most don't care for, crowded, stinky, bothersome parts. There are some parts that most can't be bothered with. And then there are a few parts that exist but are overlooked by almost everyone—mysterious places that maps leave off and minds seem to not recognize. The mesa that Witherwood sat upon was just such a part. Now, as Tobias and Charlotte sat facing Orrin, they were dreading the part they were being forced to play.*

O rrin questioned the children for over half an hour. He asked them normal questions like "How old are you?" He asked them less normal questions like "Are you allergic to any animals?" And he asked them completely ridiculous questions like "Have you ever gotten sick while riding an amusement park ride?"

"What kind of question is that?" Charlotte asked.

"It is an unusual question, but a question just the same," he reminded them. "Just answer please."

"I'd rather not," Charlotte said.

Orrin scribbled something on a piece of paper and stood up. He stretched, giving both children a clear view of the yellow sweat stains under his armpits. He dropped his arms and cleared his throat.

"We don't get many surprise students," he said, staring at Tobias. "We are very selective and have a strict...approval process."

"Then maybe we should just go," Tobias said.

"I don't think so," Orrin replied, vigorously scratching at the rash on his right arm. "It is wonderful to have you here. Besides, we could use your help."

"Help?" Charlotte asked. "The sign outside said this was a school."

"Don't believe everything you read."

"So this isn't a school?" Tobias asked.

"Of course Witherwood is a school." Orrin nodded. "It's actually a great institute of scientific learning. And I must say, it seems fortuitous that you dropped in when you did."

"Fortuitous?" Charlotte mumbled in disbelief.

"I know, it's a big word for a kid," Orrin said patronizingly. "No need for you to use it. I believe certain words are for certain ages. You may want to stick to a vocabulary more suited to your age."

"So this is a school that believes in bad vocabulary?" Tobias jumped in.

"This is an institution that believes in furthering the cause of science and wonder. We are not a dictionary."

"That makes no sense," Charlotte pointed out.

"Ah, children." Orrin stared at Charlotte with his mixed eyes. "You both seem nice, honest. But you're really just young and . . . well, that's about it. I suppose your smaller arms can reach behind cabinets to get things that have fallen, but I'm not sure what else you offer. Yes, I hate to say it—I'm afraid youth is wasted on the ignorant."

Orrin took a few minutes to preach to the Eggers kids about the importance of being obedient. It was a typical grown-up sermon that left Tobias and Charlotte feeling even more desperate and unhappy about where they were. When he was finished, Orrin stood up, smiled, and told them to follow.

Like an ugly dungeon master, Orrin retrieved a set of keys from one of his front pockets. He jingled the keys and then pinched a gold one with his index finger and thumb. He stepped over to a trophy case and slid the glass front open. With his right hand, he pushed a loose tile on the wall and exposed a keyhole.

"We'd go through the main hall," Orrin explained, "but there's something going on in there that we should probably avoid."

Orrin stuck the key in the hole and turned. The lock clicked, and he pulled open the back of the trophy case, exposing a large doorway.

"That would be kinda cool if I wasn't so scared," Charlotte whispered to Tobias.

"I agree," her brother whispered back.

Orrin turned and looked at them. "There are many things here that might surprise you. I'm still learning of new halls and closets. Of course you'll not need to bother with such things. Watch your head as we step down."

The three of them walked through the hidden door. Charlotte stayed right behind her brother, holding on to the back of his hoodie as if it were her lifeline.

The trophy case was an entrance into a large room that had much more character than the office. The space was filled with filing cabinets—hundreds of them lined the walls and were stacked throughout the room, creating a maze. The cabinets were different colors and sizes, and all had white labels on the front of the doors and drawers with letters and symbols scribbled in black marker. The ceiling was covered in pressed tin with images of stars and planets.

"What's this room?" Tobias asked.

"That's not important. In fact it's probably best you pretend it's not even here. That's what I do when things are none of my business. Now, let's keep walking."

After six turns through two different rows of cabinets, they arrived at a black door that was tall and thin. Orrin took his key and unlocked it. He bowed and pushed the door open so that Tobias and Charlotte could go first. Tobias stepped through and found himself in a stone corridor that ran alongside a large open courtyard.

"This area is called the gardens," Orrin said. "Such a beautiful spot. The school was built around it. It is an important part of Witherwood."

The gardens were like a giant courtyard, larger than six football fields, with the massive school buildings on all four sides. The school halls seemed a little like stone arms wrapped around the space. Hundreds of cottonwood trees stretched up into the yellow sky, their branches spreading out like leafy nets. Beneath the trees, large purple bushes circled a running fountain. There were two short statues near the edge of the courtyard, one of a man in a uniform and the other of a man hefting a sword into the air. Old

iron lampposts lined most of the paths that wound through the gardens. One lamppost had a small banner hanging from it that read STUDENT MORALE DAY.

The space reminded Tobias of Central Park in New York City. Tobias had never been there, but his parents had visited many years ago, and his mother had sent him a postcard with Central Park on the front of it. Tobias could still remember what she had scribbled on the back.

*Wish you were here.*

Tobias wished the same thing of her now.

Orrin instructed Tobias and Charlotte to move faster. They passed a large group of kids sitting on a metal bench at the edge of a dirt path near the fountain. The children were wearing school uniforms, the boys with ties and the girls with skirts. The students looked up and instantly began to whisper and point in their direction.

"As I was saying," Orrin told them. "You two will be a curiosity for some time. Just arrived, and already you're the talk of the school."

The three of them followed the outdoor corridor that ran along Severe Hall until they reached the far side of the gardens. They entered through a red door with CAFETERIA painted on it. Inside there were high, vaulted ceilings and rows of polished tables made of dark wood. It looked like the inside of a church that worshipped eating. The tables were empty, and the room hummed, thanks to large metal freezers against the wall. Charlotte pointed to a giant stained-glass window with the image of a puffy blue animal on it. Tobias nodded and sniffed. The air smelled like pine cleaner and bread.

"Ms. Gulp!" Orrin hollered. "Ms. Gulp!"

A red-haired woman stuck her head out of a door near the tables. "Hold your pants," she yelled, disappearing behind the door again.

"Ms. Gulp will take you to the back of Weary Hall," Orrin said. "Enter the seventh door on the left. Do you understand?"

Tobias and Charlotte nodded.

"I'm not going with you," Orrin said, scratching at his arm. "Sadly, I've got things to take care of. Ms. Gulp will find a place for you. Yes, it's true she had some sort of accident as a child. I believe she tripped while running around a pool. So her words and advice don't always make the most sense."

Charlotte nodded.

"Of course pool safety is no laughing matter," Orrin added.

Neither of them was laughing.

"Anyway, the seventh door is your room. Best not to touch any of the other doors. Go into the seventh door, pick out two beds that don't look like they are being used, and stay put until someone comes for you."

Both children nodded.

"If you leave that room before instructed, you'll find yourselves in an uncomfortable pinch," Orrin warned them. "Stay put."

"Is there a bathroom?" Tobias asked sincerely.

"Of course there's a bathroom," Orrin said. "A school without bathrooms? That's just wrong. It's behind the sixth door."

"So can we open the sixth door?" Charlotte asked.

Orrin looked confused. "Yes, Ms. Gulp will give you a chance to wash up. But don't try anything foolish. There are eyes in places you might not expect."

"But there are no eyes in the bathroom, right?" Charlotte asked.

"No more questions, please. I'm having a hard time thinking straight. Ms. Gulp!"

A big, box-shaped woman busted out of the door, mumbling, "I said I was coming."

The woman looked like a package that nobody would want to sign for. She was wearing clear rubber gloves and made a creaking noise whenever she moved. She was taller than Tobias and had red hair that was pinned back with two big clips. The top half of her was bulkier than her large lower half. There was nothing noteworthy about her appearance, besides the fact that she was wearing a brown blouse and an ugly blue skirt.

"They're all yours," Orrin said. "We'll keep them in Weary Hall for the time being, seventh door."

"Of course," she said.

Orrin waved good-bye, and Tobias and Charlotte followed Ms. Gulp over and through a wide stone arch that framed the entrance to a long hallway. The walls were marble and lined with narrow storage lockers. The floor was covered with a plush burgundy carpet.

Ms. Gulp creaked down the hall with the Eggers kids following. Her wide behind stretched across the hall, causing Tobias and Charlotte to look anywhere but forward as they walked. When Ms. Gulp passed a set of stairs leading to the second floor, she stopped to let them catch up.

"Can you walk less slowish?" she prodded. "I'm old, and I'm not struggling."

"We're not struggling," Tobias argued. "We're right behind you."

He hadn't meant it to be a joke, but Charlotte laughed when he said the word *behind*.

"Youth," Ms. Gulp said with no emotion. She then began to walk and creak again.

Past the stairs, there were some brown leather couches and a large stone fireplace. A small fire was burning in its belly and making everything hot and uncomfortable. The huge school seemed eerily empty.

The hall became thinner while the carpet got thicker. The walls were covered with pictures and certificates. One wall had a poorly painted picture of a fat man sitting on a chair. Below the picture was a small gold plaque that read HYRUM WITHERS.

"Like Witherwood?" Charlotte asked Ms. Gulp.

"Did someone tell you to look at the pictures?"

"No," Charlotte said, embarrassed. "But—"

"Butts are for smacking," Ms. Gulp said, cutting Charlotte off. "Keep your eyesight to yourself at all times. Now come on. Put the lead into it."

They walked down the hallway, passing a door about every thirty feet. All the doors were wood and matched the ones at the front of the school. Each had an eagle on it, holding something different—a pencil, a stalk of wheat, an arrow. One was holding what looked like a telescope.

Carved on the sixth door was an eagle carrying a bucket in its talons. Ms. Gulp allowed Tobias and Charlotte a few minutes to wash up in the bathroom behind it. The washroom was much bigger than any they had seen before. There were a few private stalls and some large stone showers with heavy blue drapes in front of them. The sinks were in the shapes of animals with porcelain feet and exaggerated mouths that functioned as the water basin. It almost felt dangerous washing up. Once they were finished, Ms. Gulp walked them to the seventh door.

It had a carving of an eagle with scissors in one talon and a ribbon in the other.

"This is your door," Ms. Gulp said. "You're not to wander. It takes two to . . . well . . . it takes two to mess things up."

She grabbed the brass doorknob and pushed the door open. Tobias and Charlotte walked slowly into the blackened room. Once they were all the way in, Ms. Gulp slammed the door and locked it, leaving them alone in the dark.

Tobias reached toward the wall and felt around. He flipped a light switch, and three yellow overhead lights snapped on. The room was longer than it was wide, with two rows of gray cots lined up against the walls. Each row had ten cots, and each cot looked uncomfortable. At the opposite end, there was a window with green curtains hanging limply.

Tobias and Charlotte walked slowly down the middle of the room, glancing around. The top half of the walls was covered in red textured wallpaper, and the bottom half had a gray wainscoting that ran around the room. The floor they were standing on was wood and looked as if it hadn't been polished in years.

"I miss our house," Tobias said.

At the foot of one of the cots, there were some shoes. Two other cots were ripped and torn up so much they looked unusable.

Tobias walked to the window and pushed the green curtains aside. The window looked out behind the school. There were too many trees for him to see much. He studied the latch and tried to open it. It would have been easy to bust open, but there were heavy bars on the outside of the glass, so it wouldn't have done any good.

He sat down on a cot directly under the window. Comforting sunlight trickled in and rested on his knees. Charlotte took a seat on the cot next to his.

"Did you see what that Gulp lady was wearing?" Tobias asked. "It looked like what Martha always wears."

"Grown-ups like boring clothes."

"I don't know," Tobias said. "Something's really off here. I need a pen to write stuff down."

"Maybe they'll pass pens out at Student Morale Day," Charlotte said sarcastically.

"I can't wait that long."

Tobias looked around the room, wishing a pen or pencil might magically appear. The dust sparkling in the rays of sunshine caught his attention.

"Wait," Tobias said, standing.

"I don't think there's anything else we can do," Charlotte reminded him.

Tobias walked to the corner of the room and lifted up one of the cots. The floor beneath it was as dusty as everything else.

He knelt and with his finger began to draw an outline in the dust. Charlotte stood up and watched over his shoulder. The dust was thick, and his finger worked like a pencil sketching black lines. Tobias tried to duplicate the map he had seen in Orrin's office. He then drew the iron gate and the parts of the gardens he could remember.

"I wish I had a pen and some paper, but this will have to do. It helps me to look at things, and we need to know where we are. Every detail could be important to getting out."

"I don't know how dust is going to save us," Charlotte said. "I want Dad. What if he came back last night and that *thing* got him?"

"I don't think that's what happened," Tobias said, standing up and looking at his rough map. "He's probably home thinking about what a great lesson he's taught us. We're going to have to get out of this ourselves."

The two Eggers kids stared at the map on the floor. It was roughly drawn, but seeing the image somehow made Witherwood more real. They weren't just in a strange room on a strange mesa. They were a part of something far more mysterious.

Neither one said anything for a moment as they let their situation settle over them. Tobias then carefully moved the cot back and hid the map.

He finally spoke. "You know, I can't stop thinking about something."

"Like when are they going to feed us?" Charlotte guessed.

"No," Tobias said as his stomach rumbled. "I mean, we could stay in here until someone comes and tells us to do something else, or we could check out door number eight. Sure, Orrin told us to stay away from other doors, but door number eight might be a way out."

"But he said there are eyes watching."

Tobias waved. "That's what grown-ups always say."

"True," Charlotte agreed.

"I mean, it seems like it'd be wrong not to take a look."

"Ms. Gulp locked us in," Charlotte reminded him.

"I can fix that."

Tobias stood and walked over to one of the ripped-up cots. There were springs at the corners, and he carefully worked one of the loose ones off. Tobias bent the end of it into an *L* shape. He held it up and smiled at his sister.

"Should I be impressed?" Charlotte asked.

"Not yet."

Witherwood was a mystery in many ways. Its purpose was a

secret that few people knew. It was built on top of a mesa that had sprouted from a meteorite. It was made of stone and hardwood—a mighty, formidable fortress. But it had pathetic old locks. At night they chained and padlocked all the outside doors. The school would have benefited greatly from electronic keys. Instead, most doors still had the original hardware made in the 1800s. It took a little time, but by simply using the bent spring, Tobias picked the lock and opened the door to their room.

"That's such a useful talent," Charlotte said.

"It's an ancient lock. Remember when I started Dad's car without a key? This was way easier."

Tobias carefully stepped out into the hall. It was quiet, and the smell of something earthy filled his nose.

"Someone's cooking broccoli," he whispered.

"Then we really have to get out of here," Charlotte said, following him. "I'm hungry, but not for broccoli."

The two of them crept up the hall to the eighth door. Carved on the front was a picture of an eagle carrying a fish. Tobias grabbed the doorknob but didn't turn it.

"What're you waiting for?" Charlotte asked.

"I don't know."

Beneath the low light of the hallway, Tobias smiled and then slowly twisted the doorknob.

# CHAPTER 9

# Door Number Nine

*Opening things can be quite interesting—you never know for sure what you might find. If you open a refrigerator, you often find food, but you also might find disappointment and mold. When you open a wallet, you might find money, or you might discover that you'll be skipping lunch. Opening a letter might bring you kind words from a loved one or maybe just another bill. But there's nothing quite as exciting as opening a door. The possibilities are endless.*

Well, the eighth door in Weary Hall was locked, so the Eggers kids didn't find anything there. And the keyhole was filled in with some kind of glue. They momentarily considered returning to their room, but Charlotte suggested they try door number nine. Unlike number eight, it opened easily.

Tobias stuck his head in and looked around. "It's just a dark room."

Charlotte nudged him forward.

"Hold on," Tobias complained. "There's a light switch."

Tobias flipped a switch on the wall. A large chandelier in the middle of the room popped as it came to life. The smell of burning ozone filled their nostrils.

"Ew," Charlotte said.

The room was beautifully decorated. Ornate dressers and chairs clung to the walls. There was an empty fireplace against the back wall and two large windows covered with heavy shutters. The most impressive feature was a massive four-poster bed sitting directly under the chandelier. It was high off the floor and made of dark wood with gold inlay. The posts had purple curtains between them that were closed, making it impossible to see if anyone was occupying the bed. A ticking noise was coming from somewhere. Charlotte looked around, taking it all in. Her eyes settled on the bed.

"I bet that's more comfortable than our cots," she whispered.

"No kidding," Tobias whispered back. "Maybe that's why Orrin didn't want us to come in here. Now I've got bed envy."

"Do you hear that clicking sound?"

Tobias crept nearer to the bed. The floor was blanketed with a thick white rug that covered everything but the edges of the room and made it look like winter. He glanced back at his sister and motioned for her to come. Tobias lifted his right foot and took a long step. He then stopped to listen. The clicking was a little louder and definitely coming from behind the curtains on the bed.

"Hello?" he said. "Is anybody in there?"

"Come on," Charlotte said. "It's just a ticking bed."

Tobias took three more steps and stopped. The closed purple curtains were now inches from his face. From behind the curtains, the clicking became louder.

As a rule, it's probably best not to touch or bother other people's things. As tempting as it can be at times, you'd be smart to not mess with your neighbor's car. There is wisdom in keeping your mitts off your friend's lunch. And people might label you a genius if they were to witness you keeping your hands to yourself while visiting a dynamite factory. Tobias, however, was not looking to be labeled a genius. For some reason, "do not touch" seemed more like an invitation to him than a warning. He lifted his right hand, grabbed one purple curtain, and tore it back.

"Ahhhhrrrrrap!"

Something blurry leapt up at him, screaming. It tackled him and sent him flying to the ground. The thing scratched and kicked as Tobias tried to shake off his surprise and fight back. Charlotte grabbed a book from one of the dressers and came running across the room, doing some screaming of her own. She hefted the book above her and threw it down against the attacker's head. The assailant hollered and rolled off Tobias, who scrambled to his feet and stood next to his sister. They both stared at the attacker as he whimpered like a baby on the floor.

"Thanks," Tobias said, breathing hard.

"No problem," Charlotte replied. "So who is it?"

Whoever he was wore old blue jeans and a puke-green sweater vest. He had long dark hair and untied shoes. After listening to him sob for a few more minutes, Tobias tried to reason with him.

"Honestly, she didn't hit you that hard."

"It was just a book," Charlotte said. "And not a particularly big one."

The attacker stopped blubbering.

"Where's my cube?"

He got onto his knees and scurried across the floor toward the object that had flown out of his hands earlier. It was a Rubik's Cube that was nowhere near being solved. He reached the cube and picked it up, acting like it was the last jewel in a jewel-powered world. He instantly began to turn and shift the squares. The familiar clicking noise returned.

Tobias cleared his throat uncomfortably.

The attacker stood up and sat on the edge of his bed. He looked at Tobias and Charlotte and spoke, still playing with the cube.

"This is my room."

"Sorry," Tobias said. "We got lost."

"Who are you?"

"I'm Tobias, and this is my sister, Charlotte. We've sorta been kidnapped."

"How does someone get sorta kidnapped?"

"Well, our dad dropped us off here, but I don't think we're supposed to stay."

"That's a new one."

"What's a new one?" Tobias asked.

"You being from outside," he replied. "Most of the things I make up in my head are from here in Witherwood."

Tobias and Charlotte looked at each other.

"We're not made up," Charlotte insisted.

"That's not new," the boy said. "The things I make up always say that."

"I hit you with a book," Charlotte reminded him.

"My imagination's done worse," he informed them. "I'm Fiddle, by the way. Of course it's not like you didn't already know that."

"We didn't," Tobias said, staring at him.

Fiddle seemed a couple years older than Tobias and smiled every time he talked. He had green eyes, and his long dark hair hung from his head like thin spaghetti. He wouldn't stop playing with the cube in his hand. He looked friendly in the way that some squirrels do. He also looked a little wild, much the way some other squirrels do.

"Your ears are different," Fiddle told Charlotte. "Interesting."

Charlotte pulled her hair forward.

"Why does your shirt say *hope*?"

It was a fair question. Charlotte seemed more likely to wear a shirt that read CONCERN or I WONDER; the word *hope* didn't fit. But Charlotte had been given the shirt a few years ago, and it brought her comfort. Not comfort in the sense that it was comfortable to wear; in fact, the shirt was too small. It was the kind of comfort that comes from a warm memory or a safe, quiet spot in a loud, hazardous world.

Fiddle stared at Charlotte for a few moments. When she didn't answer his question, he turned his gaze to Tobias. "So why are you in my room?"

"Shouldn't you know?" Tobias asked, still curious about being called imaginary. "If you made us up, we shouldn't be a surprise."

"You're not," Fiddle said. "I heard you call out, but I hear so many voices, I'm never sure who to believe."

"Well, do you know where a phone is?" Tobias asked.

"What's that?"

"You don't know what a phone is?" Charlotte asked, confused. "You call people with it."

Fiddle lay back on his bed and continued to fidget with the puzzle cube. "I don't know where one of those is."

"So why do you have this nice room?" Charlotte asked. "Ours is awful."

"I have this room because of my last name."

"And what's your last name?" Tobias asked.

"I forget at the moment, but my uncle says it's a good one."

"Who's your uncle?"

"He lives in that square building," Fiddle answered. "The one in the middle of the gardens. He always says, 'Fiddle, you are placed where you are because of your name.' Maybe my last name is Nicebedroom."

"Fiddle Nicebedroom?" Charlotte laughed.

"Nope, that's not it," Fiddle said, sighing. "I think it starts with an upside-down M. Did you guys know I sleepwalk?"

Both the Eggers kids shook their heads.

"I'm not positive I do, but my uncle has mentioned there's something wrong with me. I'm trying to figure out what it is."

"Maybe they should lock your door," Tobias suggested. "I'm not sure it's a good idea for us to be sleeping so close to your room."

"You can't be too safe," Fiddle agreed.

"We should go," Charlotte said to her brother. "I don't want them to notice that we're missing."

"Yeah," Fiddle said. "Beware of the voices."

"Like in your head?" Tobias asked.

"No." Fiddle laughed. "The voices! The guards who walk the halls at night and sing. My uncle says the singing keeps things at bay, but I don't know what that means. I guess the dark makes the mesa a little dangerous, and the music helps. Lots of times I can hear the voices singing as they pass my door. I'll tell you this—the songs they pick are pretty awful."

"It seems foolish to be a singing night watchman," Charlotte said. "People will always hear you coming."

"They're not worried about people inside. I think they're more interested in what's on the outside of Witherwood. Have you seen the chains they use to lock things up at night?"

Tobias and Charlotte nodded.

"That's because something went wrong."

It's a fact of life that sometimes things go wrong. Most people don't make it through an entire day without something happening that shouldn't have. But when you're trapped in a strange place talking to a strange person, the phrase "something went wrong" is particularly unsettling.

"What happened?" Tobias asked.

"Something with the animals outside. It's okay now."

It didn't feel okay.

"Don't listen to me," Fiddle said kindly. "There are good things to be found here." He sat up, dropped his Rubik's Cube, and instantly began twisting a loose string that was coming off the worn knee hole on his jeans. "For example, I know something nice."

"Something nice and useful?" Tobias asked, picking up the Rubik's Cube.

Fiddle looked confused. His forehead wrinkled, and his eyes grew squinty. "Maybe I'm not sure what I know," he finally answered.

"We really should go," Charlotte said once more.

Tobias quickly twisted and solved the Rubik's Cube. He tossed it back to Fiddle, who stared at it in awe.

The Eggers kids turned and headed for the door.

"Wait," Fiddle shouted. "I remember what I know. There's a door somewhere."

"That door?" Tobias asked, pointing to a small door at the far end of Fiddle's room.

"No, that's my bathroom."

"You've got your own bathroom?" Charlotte asked jealously.

"I don't like sharing," Fiddle admitted.

"Forget about the bathroom. What door are you talking about?" Tobias asked.

"The door off the mesa," Fiddle replied. "I—"

The bedroom door flew open. Standing in the doorway was Ms. Gulp. Her gloved hands were reaching out. Her face was as red as her hair.

Fiddle screamed.

"What are you doing in here?" Ms. Gulp snapped. "I thought I locked your door."

"It wasn't locked," Tobias lied. "We went to the bathroom and came back to the wrong room."

"Door number seven is your door. What kind of children can't count to seven? I think you're being curious, and curiosity flattened the cat."

"That's true," Fiddle confirmed.

"We're sorry," Charlotte apologized.

"I'm sure you are," she snipped. "Now come!"

"Wait," Fiddle said. "I was about to tell them something."

"Sorry, Fiddle," she replied. "You'll have to save it for later. These two children need to get their sleep so they don't wake up on the wrong side of the room."

Fiddle shrugged. "Okay. Good-bye, imaginations. Oh, and, Ms. Gulp, they suggested you might want to lock my door. You know, to be safe."

Tobias looked down at the white rug, wishing he hadn't opened his mouth.

"Thank you, Fiddle," Ms. Gulp said. "We'll start locking it straightaway."

Ms. Gulp led Tobias and Charlotte to their room. She asked them a bunch of barely understandable questions, gave them a little information, and warned them to behave. She also let them know that she wouldn't forget to use the lock this time.

"You might want to lie down and take a nap. You will be picked up for service in about three hours."

"What kind of service?" Charlotte asked.

"Dinner service. We'll start you in the kitchen. We have extra menus and work to complete before the parade next week. Student Morale Day means a lot of extra work for me."

"Sorry," Charlotte said.

"That doesn't help."

"So, where are the other students?" Tobias asked. "The ones who sleep on these other cots?"

"They've graduated. Now, lie down."

"Are there any blankets and pillows?" Charlotte asked.

"Plenty," Ms. Gulp answered.

"Could we get some?"

Ms. Gulp laughed, and spittle flew from her mouth. "We don't just hand blankets and pillows out," she said with disgust. "You'll have to earn them. And you can start earning them this evening in the kitchen."

Ms. Gulp took her large, boxy body and interesting speech skills and left the room. She slammed the door behind her, and it clicked.

"I don't like Ms. Gulp," Charlotte whispered.

"More like Big Gulp," Tobias added.

"Well, I don't like Big Gulp," Charlotte said. "I can't understand half of what she's talking about. She almost makes me miss Orrin. We have to get out of here."

"I know, and I think Fiddle might know how."

"I don't think Fiddle knows anything," Charlotte said sadly.

Tobias yawned. "I think he does, and we'll ask him as soon as we can, but right now I'm going to sleep."

Charlotte yawned even wider as she lay down on her cot.

"Do you think Dad is worried about us?" she asked drowsily.

Tobias was already asleep.

# CHAPTER 10

# STARTING FROM SCRATCHES

R alph Eggers slowly opened his eyes. A flood of white light was covering his body. He blinked twice and then snapped his eyelids shut again.

"Hello?" A soft voice beckoned.

He opened his eyes to see an angel in a nurse's uniform standing beside him. He displayed a weak smile while she showed off one of her strongest grins.

"You're awake," she said happily. "Let me get the doctor."

The beautiful nurse hurried off, leaving Ralph alone. He peered down and saw the tube running into his left wrist and the thin beige blanket covering his body. He tried to lift his right arm to scratch an itch on his forehead, but his arm wouldn't cooperate. In fact, it was in a white cast and impossible to move.

Ralph Eggers looked around the room, wondering where he was and if he was even awake. A big machine next to his bed beeped a few times and then went silent. He wiggled his toes and shifted his legs under the blanket. There was a small TV up in the corner. The sound was off, but on the screen was a woman wearing a shawl and holding a bird—looking at the picture made him more confused.

The beautiful nurse with the soft voice came back, a gray-haired man trailing behind her. "Doctor," she said nicely, "our patient's awake."

"That's good to see," the doctor replied. "How do you feel?"

"Fine," Ralph said. "My head hurts a little."

"That's not surprising. You sustained a minor concussion—nothing too serious. And as you probably noticed, your arm's broken but it was a clean break and should heal well."

"That's good," Ralph said. "So what happened to me?"

The doctor smiled the way doctors do when they need to say something unpleasant in a pleasant way.

"We're not sure. You were found walking through the desert this morning by a rancher. He said you were speaking incoherently and staggering around. He thought you had been drinking, but the tests show there's no alcohol in your system. You were pretty scratched up. The rancher brought you here, and we put

your arm in a cast. We were actually hoping you'd be able to tell us what happened."

Ralph Eggers looked down at his left arm. He could see a couple of small scratches and a long, finger-wide bruise.

"So—" The doctor stopped to look at the chart. "Oh, that's right. We don't even have your name." He clicked his pen and held it over the chart in preparation for writing. "Now, what is your name?"

Ralph Eggers looked at the beautiful nurse and then at the gray-haired doctor.

"I have no idea."

"Really?" the doctor asked.

"It's like I can't remember anything," Ralph replied.

For the first time since he had opened his eyes, the beautiful nurse frowned. Her expression fit the feeling that was growing in Ralph's gut.

"Do you know what year it is?" the doctor asked.

Ralph shook his head.

"Do you have any family?"

"I don't . . . think so," Ralph said slowly.

"Can you tell me how old you are?"

Ralph looked down at his body as he lay in bed. "I'm sorry, no."

"The rancher who found you wandering said you didn't have a wallet. In fact, you were practically naked."

"What?" Ralph said, confused.

"You had no shirt, no shoes, and your pants were so badly ripped they were barely hanging on you."

"That's not good, is it?" Ralph asked.

"I'm afraid not," the doctor answered.

The doctor then picked up a phone as Ralph Eggers closed his eyes and tried desperately to remember something. Anything.

# CHAPTER 11

# WAKING UP IS HARD TO DO

*No sleep is no fun. I suppose playing tag all night can be okay, but when your body realizes that it's missed a night of slumber, things get unpleasant. Nobody enjoys being around someone who is lacking a full eight hours' worth. And nobody enjoys being the one who lacks it. There is only one case where less sleep is acceptable. That is the case that involves you reading this book and not setting it down and dozing off. But aside from that, no sleep is no fun.*

Tobias had no desire to get up. Unfortunately, what he desired had nothing to do with what was happening. As he was lying on his cot dreaming about maps and mechanics, Ms. Gulp violently shook his shoulder and commanded him to get up.

"Just one more hour," he slurred.

"Get moving!" she snapped. "Nap's over."

"Please," he begged, his eyes refusing to open. "Let me sleep half an hour more."

Ms. Gulp grabbed the side of Tobias's cot and yanked it straight up. Tobias flew out and came crashing down against the floor.

"Ow," he complained as he sat up. He looked at the overturned cot and wished he were still in it.

"Now wake your sister and come with me," Ms. Gulp ordered. "We've a lot to do."

Tobias looked at Charlotte. She was still sleeping peacefully on her cot. "Why didn't you wake her up first?"

Ms. Gulp grabbed Tobias by the left ear and pinched. "Get your sister and come. I've got responsibilities calling my number."

Ms. Gulp let go of Tobias's ear and walked out the door into the hall.

It took Tobias five very hard shakes to wake Charlotte. She was even less pleased about being awakened than he had been.

"I'm so tired."

"You have to get up," Tobias whispered. "Big Gulp's pinching."

"Big Gulp's pinching," Charlotte slurred incoherently.

"Get her up!" Ms. Gulp yelled from the door.

Tobias pulled his sister to her feet. Charlotte swayed for a few seconds and then slid back down onto her cot.

"I wanna sleep," she cried groggily.

"Me too," Tobias said as Ms. Gulp stomped back across the room. "But you've got to get up now!"

It was too late. Ms. Gulp grabbed Charlotte by the nape of her neck, hoisted her onto her feet, and marched her across the room and out into the hall. Charlotte was yelling while trying to fully understand what was happening. Tobias hurried after them, but Ms. Gulp kept him at bay, kicking her fat left leg back and swatting with her free arm.

"Let her go!" he yelled.

Ms. Gulp pushed Charlotte into the large bathroom behind door number six. She placed Charlotte in one of the stone showers behind the blue curtains and turned on the cold water full blast. Tobias was still trying to get to his sister, so Ms. Gulp grabbed his arm and shoved him into the shower too.

"Tell me when you're awake," she barked.

"I'm awake!" Charlotte yelled.

"Me too," Tobias added.

"Are you sure?" Ms. Gulp asked.

Both kids stood under the cold water, looking as pathetic

as they had when they first arrived. Their teeth chattered. Ms. Gulp turned the spigot and shut the water off. She smiled at them.

"Let me guess," Tobias chattered. "You have to earn your towels."

"What a smart young man you are!" she said.

Tobias and Charlotte shook themselves until they were no longer dripping. Tobias took off his red hoodie and wrung out as much water as he could. He put it back on and shivered from his toes to the top of his forehead. Ms. Gulp handed them a used rag.

"Hurry," Ms. Gulp barked. "Better not late than ever."

"We wouldn't be late if you hadn't . . ." Tobias saw Ms. Gulp's red face and decided to stop talking.

They took turns with the rag, trying their best to dry off their faces and arms. Completely defeated, they followed Ms. Gulp into the hallway, through the halls, and over to the large cathedral-like cafeteria. Behind the cafeteria, through two swinging wood doors, was a cavernous old kitchen.

The walls were covered in yellow tiles that had probably begun their journey in life white. The floorboards curled slightly at the edges, making it hard to walk without tripping. There were a number of stoves and ovens and three massive fireplaces with heavy iron pots hanging over lit fires. Butcher-block tables as long as the room ran through the middle of the kitchen and were covered with various foods. The far wall was lined with a row of dirty sinks that resembled antique bathtubs someone had forgotten to scrub. An opening in the wall near one of the fireplaces led to the dark kitchen cellar. The place smelled like fresh meat, stale potatoes, and cocoa.

"Has anyone cleaned this place since 1805?" Tobias asked.

"That's why you're here," Ms. Gulp said smugly.

Ms. Gulp gave them a list of jobs longer than any list they had ever seen. Both wanted to complain but were scared to say anything for fear of being shoved into another shower or thwacked on the ear.

Tobias and Charlotte spent the next three hours scrubbing pots and cleaning the counters and floors in the kitchen. They were also in charge of bringing food up from the cellar. As they worked, they could hear the din of students out at the tables eating their dinner. Women in brown blouses and blue skirts carried food out from the kitchen, then returned with empty trays for Tobias and Charlotte to clean. They wanted to peek out and see the other students, but every time they tried to get close to one of the doors, Ms. Gulp would stop them.

"Do as you're told and not a thing more!"

When the cafeteria was empty, Tobias and Charlotte were allowed out of the kitchen to bus the tables and wash the remaining dishes. Following that, Ms. Gulp served them each a plate with two pieces of bread, a smashed potato with some sort of mustard squirted over it, half an apple, and a jar of chocolate pudding. Tobias and Charlotte sat at one of the empty wood tables and ate what they had been given. It was their first meal since they had arrived. It wasn't what they would have ordered if they had had a choice, but it felt good just to eat something. Their hands were raw from washing dishes, and their arms were tired and sticky, but they didn't let any of that stop them from eating. Through the stained-glass window they could see that the sky was dark.

"I wish I was dreaming all this," Charlotte said as she finished her second piece of bread. "My insides feel like a giant bruise."

Tobias wanted to tell his sister that everything was going to be all right, but he wasn't sure things actually would be. "This pudding's good."

"Yeah," Charlotte said, taking a big bite of hers. "But I'm not staying at Witherwood for the pudding."

"It has an unusual smell," Tobias noted.

"Still not staying," Charlotte reiterated. "Ms. Gulp keeps complaining about Student Morale Day, and I don't want to be here when it comes. It sounds awful."

"Listen," Tobias whispered, trying to comfort her. "I'll get us out."

"When?" Charlotte asked, her lips covered with pudding.

"Tonight," Tobias answered. "I have an idea."

Charlotte slipped her last bite of apple into her mouth.

"Putting the tadpoles in the gravy was an idea of yours. So was getting out of Dad's car."

"This idea's different," Tobias insisted.

Ms. Gulp came out of the kitchen. It looked like she had just eaten a big plate of leftovers without using her hands. She smacked her messy lips and instructed the kids to follow her back to their room. And even though there was nobody around besides the three of them, she ordered them not to talk to anyone.

"Understand? Also, you'll be needed in the kitchen tomorrow."

"What about school?" Charlotte asked. "Isn't there a school here?"

"I told you not to talk to anyone," Ms. Gulp scolded.

"Not even you?"

"Especially me."

As they passed the large set of stairs, Tobias could see a light at the top shining out from beneath a solid wood door.

"What's on the second floor?" Tobias asked.

"No talking."

"Is that where the other students are?"

"You worry about where you belong," Ms. Gulp commanded. "Remember, do as you're told and not a thing more."

Tobias and Charlotte were quiet. When they reached their room, Ms. Gulp shut their door and locked it behind them. Tobias flipped the switch and the lights came on.

"So who do you like more?" Tobias asked his sister. "Martha or Big Gulp?"

"Neither," Charlotte replied. "I like Orrin and his rashy skin and mismatched eyes."

Tobias smiled, and for a second, all the horrible things happening to them felt light.

"Why won't they let us see the other students?" Tobias said. "And what's so special about the second floor?"

"I don't care," Charlotte answered. "I'm tired, and I want out."

When they reached their cots, they saw that folded on the ends of them were a couple of blankets.

"I know you have a plan," Charlotte said softly. "But those blankets look soft. Maybe we should take a quick nap."

"No, we really need to go now. They won't be looking for us. Besides, if we fall asleep, we'll never get up."

"But we have blankets," Charlotte moaned. "And we're tired."

"I'd be happy to throw you in the shower," Tobias offered.

Charlotte sat down on the edge of her cot. "Fine. What's the plan?"

Tobias smiled and then slowly pulled something out of the pocket of his hoodie.

# CHAPTER 12

# A First Look at Floor Two

*People usually have some idea of what's coming next. Few people are surprised when they put money into a soda machine and soda comes out. Likewise, most people aren't caught off guard when they drive a car and it runs out of gas. And there is certainly no element of surprise when you put an assailant into a dryer and he comes out hot under the collar.*

Knowing Tobias and having heard hundreds of his plans over the years, Charlotte thought she wouldn't be surprised by what Tobias had planned. She was wrong.

"That's it?" Charlotte asked in amazement. "That's your plan?"

"What?" Tobias said defensively. "It could work." He was holding a pair of pliers he'd taken from the kitchen. "Watch."

Tobias retrieved another spring from the ripped-up cot. This time, with the pliers, he was able to bend and shape the spring into what looked like a homemade key. He kept at it, testing different shapes in the lock on their door until...

*Click.*

"I saw Orrin's and Ms. Gulp's big keys and figured I could make one of my own. I bet this will open most of the doors in Witherwood. Old locks are easy."

"So you've picked the lock. What next?"

"We go to Fiddle. He knows something. You heard him say there was a door."

"There are lots of doors," Charlotte pointed out.

"He wasn't talking about a normal door. He said off the mesa."

"Right," she moaned. "But even if we do get out through some door, what about that thing outside?"

"I've been thinking about that," Tobias said. "What if it was fake, just something to frighten us from leaving?"

"Something fake tore your shoe and chased us up a tree? Are you forgetting it was vicious?"

"It could have been fake," Tobias insisted. "Someone dressed up so that we'd have to come back and do their dishes. We were tricked. I bet that scream we heard when we first met Orrin was just a recording. He probably pressed a button or something to set it off."

"This is crazy," Charlotte said. "You're tired and not making any sense. I'm going to sleep."

"All right, stay here then," Tobias offered. "I'll talk to Fiddle and then come back."

"Wait! I don't want to stay alone."

"Then come."

Tobias hid the pliers beneath a loose floorboard in the corner of their room. He walked back and slowly pulled open the bedroom door. The hallway was empty. He glanced at his sister as she sat on her cot, looking as tired as he felt.

"Come on," he whispered kindly. "I need your ears to listen for singing, and if we do find a way out of this place, we can sleep forever in real beds."

Charlotte gave in and joined her brother.

The plush carpet in the hallway kept their footsteps muffled. They walked past door number eight and up to number nine. Tobias used the key, and the door unlocked. He pushed it open and gazed into the dark room.

"He's gone," Charlotte said.

"How can you tell?"

"The sound. If he's in there, he's not breathing."

"And he no longer smells like he did," Tobias said.

Tobias reached in and flipped on the light. The curtains around Fiddle's bed were drawn but he wasn't there. They checked the bathroom. Empty as well.

"I hope he's okay," Charlotte said.

"Me too. Without him we don't know where the door is."

"So far your plan isn't working," Charlotte whispered.

Tobias looked at his tired sister. The way her nose twitched and her deep eyes blinked reminded him of their mother. The mother who was no longer alive to worry about them. All the things they were going through never would have happened if their mom hadn't died. Both of them knew this, and both of them knew there was no point in bringing it up. Death had snuck into their lives and taken their happiness.

"You remember those old barns back behind our house?" Tobias whispered.

Charlotte nodded.

"Remember how scared we were to explore them?"

More nodding.

"But when we did, we found cool stuff—that hammer and that old engine. This is just like exploring those barns."

"We weren't locked up in those barns. And nobody was watching us."

"So this will be even more exciting," Tobias cheered quietly. "We need to explore. Something's going on here, and as much as I want to escape, I also want to find out what that is."

Tobias turned and left Fiddle's room. He walked with his back to the wall, and Charlotte fell in line next to him. When they got to a set of stairs leading up to the second floor, he stopped.

"Wait! We're going up?" Charlotte asked. "Shouldn't we be looking for a way out?"

"We know what's out that way—Never Hall, Ms. Gulp, Orrin, weird animals. But we don't know what's upstairs. Maybe the windows aren't barred. Maybe that's where the other students sleep and they can help us. Plus, we need more information for my map."

Tobias began to climb the stairs, and without further fuss, Charlotte followed. The door at the top was locked, but the key Tobias had made worked perfectly.

"You make a great criminal," Charlotte said.

They slipped past the door, shutting it behind them. The second floor was dark, but their eyes adjusted and things came quickly into focus.

Ten feet away from them was a reception desk, and behind the desk were bookshelves loaded with papers and messy files. The area looked more like a hospital than a school and didn't match the first floor at all. Down the hall in both directions was darkness.

"Creepy," Charlotte whispered.

Tobias walked behind the reception desk and grabbed the handle of one of the drawers. The first was empty, but the second had just what he needed—pens. There were two of them, and Tobias took both. He slipped them into his pockets and checked the other drawers. All empty.

"Um, Tobias," Charlotte whispered.

Tobias looked up as he softly closed the last drawer.

"I think I hear someone singing."

They crept slowly down the long hallway, listening. They passed dozens of closed doors with numbers on them. They tested each door, but all were locked. There were posters on the walls of friendly-looking animals and sayings like *Every dog has his day* and *Don't pity the kitty*.

Tobias paid special attention to what he saw so that he could write it down later. The hallway turned, and in view was an empty kitchen and two fireplaces. Passing the kitchen, Tobias finally heard the singing.

"I think it's coming from the third floor," Charlotte whispered.

"We should find some stairs going up," Tobias suggested.

"I'd rather find some going out."

After twenty more steps, there was an alcove with another empty desk. A window behind the desk was facing the gardens and made the area a little lighter than the rest of the floor. There were no bars on the window.

On the other side of the alcove was an open door. Without saying a word to each other, they walked through the door into a cramped room that smelled like cleaning supplies and eggs. There was a dry mop in the corner, and buckets filled with liquid on the floor. Metal shelves sat along the wall.

"Wait," Charlotte whispered. "Someone's coming."

Tobias closed the door so there was only a small crack to peek out of. The hallway was dark, but someone was pushing something squeaky and getting closer. As it passed the door the Eggers kids were hiding behind, they saw a man in a yellow lab coat pushing a wheelchair with a person in it. He was singing softly:

> There is no up, and there's no down.
> The world may stop from spinning round.
> Tomorrow there'll be light, they say,
> So rest up now, and we will see.

Tobias and Charlotte held their breath as the singing man continued down the hall and into the dark.

"Did you hear that?" Tobias asked in disbelief.

The song was one that Mrs. Eggers had sung to her children

almost every night before they went to bed. The night before she died, she had sung it to both of them. Charlotte had dozed off as she did. Tobias had complained about being too old for lullabies.

"I want out," Charlotte said nervously. "I hear too many sounds, and I'm so tired I can't think straight. We need—"

Charlotte was interrupted by the sound of an intercom snapping to life in the hallway. The crackling filled the air. They both put their hands up over their ears.

"Attention, participants." It was Orrin. "It seems as if we are missing a couple of new wards. The boy and the girl have mistakenly stepped from their room. If seen, they should be directed to where they belong. Thank you."

The intercom snapped off. Tobias and Charlotte stared at each other.

"Not good," Tobias whispered.

He took his sister's hand, and they walked back out into the hallway. They could hear doors opening in the distance.

"The window," Tobias said.

They climbed behind the empty desk, and Tobias grabbed the latch on the window. It slid open easily, and the smells and sounds of the courtyard gardens drifted in. Tobias pushed out the screen and leaned over the windowsill. There were trees and some bushes directly below.

"We have to jump," he insisted.

Charlotte was already climbing out the window. She twisted and hung down from the windowsill. She then kicked out and tumbled to the tall hedge, making it look easy.

"Great," Tobias said, wishing he was as coordinated as his sister.

He carefully climbed out and slowly lowered himself until he was hanging from the windowsill. His fingers burned as he struggled to hold on.

There were voices coming from inside.

Tobias did his best to push out, but his legs couldn't kick hard enough, and as he let go, his right arm scratched up against the stone wall. He bounced backward and landed on his bent knees in a bush that was more abrasive than soft. He might have stayed stuck there forever if not for Charlotte. She was right next to him, yanking him out.

"Are you okay?"

"Fine," Tobias said, embarrassed. "Let's go."

They crouched low and moved along a thin dirt trail toward the center of the gardens. The area was dark; waves of light were drifting out from the metal lampposts like sparks from a lazy wand. The light illuminated pockets of trees and created menacing shadows.

Charlotte gasped.

"What are those?" she asked nervously.

Above them in the branches were twelve sets of glowing eyes. The eyes were big and were attached to round bodies the size of basketballs. One set of eyes jiggled as a mouth opened beneath, revealing two rows of jagged teeth.

Charlotte started to scream, and Tobias covered her mouth with his hand. "Quiet," he whispered. "Those probably aren't even real. Remember, they're trying to trick us. Look how fake they—"

All at once, the twelve sets of glowing eyes leapt down toward them. Tobias could feel teeth digging into his right shoulder as claws tore through his left arm. He grabbed Charlotte and charged directly through the middle of the trees and across the gardens. He swatted one of the creatures from his head as Charlotte shook one off that was attempting to bite her leg.

"Hurry!" he yelled.

As they ran, the gardens seemed to come alive. Screams and wailing like they had never heard before filled their ears. Animals emerged from the foliage and jumped down from the trees above and behind them.

"Well?" Charlotte yelled.

"Well, what?" Tobias asked, breathing at least twice as hard as his sister.

"Don't try to tell me those aren't real animals or that they're just adults dressed up in costumes."

"No," Tobias heaved. "Those are real."

"That means whatever chased us last night was probably real too!"

Tobias jumped into a short tunnel that ran beneath a massive stone. He popped out the other side and kept running alongside Charlotte. They stumbled through a Student Morale Day banner hanging from the side of a lamppost and fell to the ground. Picking themselves up, they continued to run until Tobias could run no more. He slipped behind a horseshoe-shaped boulder and ducked as low as he could. Charlotte crouched next to him as something about the size of an orange landed on Tobias's head and began to tear at his hair. With one strong nod, he threw his head to the side and smacked the creature against the boulder. The animal bellowed and fell to the ground.

"Look," Charlotte whispered. "It's so little."

The creature shook and cried.

"I think you broke its . . . wing?"

"It was tearing at my head," Tobias whispered back.

The wounded creature sputtered and rolled on its side. Without thinking, Charlotte reached out and picked it up. The animal was covered in stringy feathers that resembled miniature dread-locks. It was round and had droopy ears and large bulging eyes perched on top of an olive-sized nose. It opened its mouth and squawked.

Tobias looked at his sister. "You can't keep it."

"We can't leave it," she whispered.

"I could give you about a hundred reasons why we should, but I know you won't listen."

"Good. Don't tell me then," Charlotte said. "We should keep going. I can hear people coming."

"I don't know where to go," Tobias admitted. "We're trapped in these gardens."

"Well then, let's find somewhere better to hide."

They moved quickly away from the horseshoe-shaped boulder and toward the middle of the gardens. Charlotte held the small creature against her chest. Eyes flashed open around them as they ran, but no animals attacked.

"Maybe it's good you kept that thing," Tobias said. "And could you please run slower? I can't breathe."

Charlotte slowed just a bit.

In the center of the gardens was a building covered in ivy. Charlotte would have run right into it while weaving through the trees if the animal in her hands hadn't squawked. She came to a skidding stop and braced herself for Tobias to slam into her. This was unnecessary—Tobias was still a good twenty feet behind and having a hard time. He caught up and attempted to catch his breath.

"What is that?" he huffed, staring at the ivy-covered structure.

"I don't remember seeing a building in the gardens on the school map."

"I think this is what Fiddle was talking about. But that doesn't matter, because I hear people."

The siblings ran around the square building, but the only door they found was locked tight. Sounds of more and more voices and footsteps were around them.

The speakers announced, "The missing students are in the gardens."

Charlotte took her brother's hand and headed toward East Hall. They wound through bushes and down a narrow dirt path that zigged across the overgrown ground. Tobias tripped, and Charlotte helped him up while still holding the animal. A stone trail led them to one of the main paths heading directly to East Hall. They could see the glass double doors.

"I have an idea," Tobias said confidently.

Searchlights snapped on and began sweeping the gardens. A large beam of light brushed past them as they pushed themselves into the bushes.

Tobias spotted a metal ladder attached to East Hall near the corner of the gardens. From where he was, it looked like the ladder went all the way to the top of the school.

"Wait, I have a new idea," Tobias said.

"Is it better than the first one?"

"Definitely. Follow me."

Tobias and Charlotte stayed beneath the cover of trees as voices and searchlights drifted over the landscape. The animal Charlotte was holding clicked and sniffed in her hands. When the lights were far enough away, they dashed quickly to where the corners of East Hall and Severe Hall met up. It was a difficult run. Twice they had to drop to the ground to hide as people in yellow lab coats passed them.

"Over there," Tobias whispered, indicating the ladder. "We'll climb to the roof. Then we can find a way down or over to the other side, or make a signal fire, or at least hide on the roof."

"Good," Charlotte said.

They crept slowly through some leafy bushes to where the ladder was attached to the wall. There was a small metal gate around the base of the ladder, and a fat padlock hung from the latch.

"Here," Charlotte said, handing Tobias the animal in her hands. "Hold Lars."

"Lars?"

"What? I like that name."

Tobias took Lars and placed him in the pocket of his hoodie as his sister jumped and grabbed the top of the metal gate. She pulled herself up and onto the ladder. Turning around, she reached down for Tobias. He took her hand and, with a little help, climbed over the metal gate and onto the ladder below Charlotte.

"Climb," he said. "Before we're spotted."

Charlotte ascended the ladder, with Tobias close behind her. They passed the second-story windows, which were dark. A few feet later, Tobias could see into one of the third-story windows. He wasn't sure, but he thought he saw a face.

One of the giant searchlights locked onto both of them, causing them to freeze. They clung to the ladder.

"Keep going!" Tobias insisted.

Charlotte would have, but above her, staring from the top of the ladder, were a couple of gruff-looking orderlies. One actually had a net. They glanced down, and Orrin was standing on the ground below with another group of orderlies.

Tobias tried to see into one of the other third-story windows. There was another face, and he heard someone moaning.

"Do you see—?"

Tobias's question was cut short as Orrin yelled up at them. "Come off that, please!"

Tobias and Charlotte stared at him.

"Quickly," Orrin said. "I don't like ladders."

"You're not on it," Tobias hollered down. "We are." He was exhausted and having a difficult time hanging on.

"Still, just the thought of it," Orrin pleaded.

They could see more people with flashlights gathering below. Some pointed their lights at them on the ladder as others questioned Orrin about what to do next. Tobias looked up at his sister as she looked down at him.

"I'm sorry," he said.

Charlotte was quiet.

Once more, Orrin begged them to climb down. This time they obeyed. As Tobias descended, he secretly tossed his homemade key into some tall bushes. He wasn't about to give up any of his secrets.

The metal gate around the bottom of the ladder had been unlocked, and as soon as Tobias stepped off the lowest rung, someone yanked him away. Another pulled Charlotte off. Lars squawked loudly. An orderly took the small creature from Tobias.

"Thank goodness you're down," Orrin said, relieved, his bald head looking ghostly in the dark. "Death by ladder would be horrible. That said, we're going to need to take you to visit someone now. Someone who's great at straightening things out."

"Things like us?" Tobias asked, trying to sound tough.

"Things exactly like you," Orrin said, smiling. "We've given you a beautiful opportunity, and it seems like you're taking advantage of us. It just breaks my heart when children don't understand what a wonderful gift they've been given."

"It breaks our hearts to be kept here," Charlotte quipped.

"Well then, I guess we all know how one another feels," Orrin said nicely. "Let the straightening begin."

# CHAPTER 13

## ERASING ONE'S MIND

Late *is a sad little word. It can mean so many things, but rarely is it used for good. If you show up late, you're tardy. If you turn in late, you're tired. If your work's late, you may be fired. If you come home late, you're grounded, and if you're the late Mr. or Ms. So-and-So, that means you've expired, kicked the bucket, gone to bunk with the dirt fairy. You've died.* Late *can affect time as well. It can be growing late, late enough, or if you're into silly wordplay, late o'clock. I feel, however, that the worst form of* late *is the dreaded* too late. *It leaves little room for hope. How can you feel good about anything when you know it's too late?*

**W**ell, it was too late for Tobias and Charlotte to feel good about anything. As they were pushed through the dark gardens toward the square building, they felt as if it was not only too late, it was too heavy. Their knees buckled under the weight of each step.

"You'll be straightened out soon enough," Orrin repeated, as if it were something they should be happy about.

For the record, no kid likes hearing those words, and no kid is happy about it when he or she does.

When they reached the square building, Orrin unlocked the door, and the two orderlies escorting the siblings shoved them through it.

Inside, yellow light washed the room in shades of autumn. The back wall was a giant mirror. In the center of the room, there was a thick gold ring on the floor that appeared to be a handle to a trapdoor. Aside from two plastic folding chairs, the room was vacant. On the long wall opposite the mirror there were some large backward-printed words. Looking in the mirror, they read

TIME IS A TRICK OF THE MIND.

"Stay here," Orrin said. "Marvin will be with you soon." He locked the door behind them.

Alone, Tobias and Charlotte stared at the mirror, barely recognizing the scratched-up, ragged kids they saw staring back at them.

"Is that really us?" Charlotte asked.

"I think so."

Tobias's hair was sticking out in numerous directions. His arms were covered in dirt, and his hoodie was ripped in two places. The freckles beneath his blue eyes looked as if they were dripping. Charlotte's jeans were torn at the ends, and the left sleeve of her green HOPE shirt was shredded.

"We look awful," Tobias added.

Charlotte's knees gave out, and she fell to the ground crying. Tobias knelt and put his arm around his sister.

"This is your fault," she whispered. "You're the older one. Aren't you supposed to know better? Now look at us."

They both stared in the mirror. It wasn't pretty.

"Dad would never have left me here if it weren't for you."

"Be careful what you say," Tobias said, growing angry.

"Or what?" Charlotte hollered. "You'll throw me into a strange school and lock me up?"

"I can't—"

Tobias stopped arguing as the yellow light above them began to dim. The mirrored wall was beginning to glow.

"Don't be afraid," a low, almost hypnotic voice told them.

The two glanced around, searching for speakers or a person.

"Who said that?" Tobias asked.

"Have a seat," the voice said. "I know how I hate to stand."

"We're not standing," Tobias pointed out as he knelt next to Charlotte.

"Quite right," the voice replied. "But a chair will be much more comfortable."

Tobias looked at the two folding chairs and then back at the glowing mirror.

"Where are we?"

"As I said, have a seat."

"Where are we?" Tobias asked the air again.

"Sit," the voice insisted.

Tobias stood and walked to the folding chairs. He picked them both up and shuffled back to Charlotte. Without warning, he spun and threw the chairs toward the mirrored wall, screaming, "Ahhhhhhhhh!"

The two chairs slammed up against the mirror and bounced off, causing no visible damage.

"Have a seat," the voice said once more.

Tobias didn't want to. He walked over to the trapdoor on the floor and pulled on the gold ring. There was no budge or wiggle.

"Are you ready to sit?" the voice said.

Beaten, Tobias retrieved the chairs and set them facing the mirror. He reached down to help Charlotte, but his sister refused the offer. She stood up by herself, and they both sat down dejectedly. Facing the glowing mirror from the sitting position, they could see just how banged up their knees were from all their climbing and running.

"We're sitting," Tobias reported.

"Perfect," the voice purred deeply. "Do you know where you are?"

They both shook their heads.

"You are in the square room," the voice informed them. "It's where I greet visitors. It's also the second structure that was built on top of the mesa. The first was a small outhouse at the back of the mesa near the spring. It would be awkward to greet visitors there."

Charlotte was trying to keep her eyes open. Something about the man's voice made her head feel heavy and pleasantly foggy.

"Keep talking," Charlotte said softly.

"My pleasure," the voice replied. "My pleasure."

Tobias's mind began to muddle up as well. "Something's going on here at Witherwood," he mumbled.

"I don't know what you are speaking of," the voice said. "Something goes on almost everywhere."

"Not something like this," Tobias said in a daze. "This isn't a real school, is it? It's like a secret. I saw some old people in the window. They were—"

"You don't need to worry about such things," the voice said. "You just need to behave. This school deserves your respect. It's quite a special place."

"What do . . ." Tobias couldn't finish his sentence, due to a feeling of haziness.

"You disobeyed and caused a commotion tonight," the voice recounted.

"Sorry," Tobias slurred.

"You disturbed my gardens," the voice said calmly.

"Still sorry," Tobias admitted.

"You worried the staff and tore one of our banners. Who knows what else you've done."

"Who knows," Tobias said innocently.

"Your voice," Charlotte tried to explain. "It's making my head heavy and I can't think straight."

"Good," the voice replied. "In a moment, your minds will be mush enough to look at me. Then we will have a real discussion."

"That's horrible," Tobias said in a dreamlike state.

"What's horrible?" the voice asked.

"What you're doing to us," Tobias slurred.

"I'd prefer to talk to you face-to-face, but that never seems to go well," the voice explained. "My parents were horrified by my appearance, and they were even more horrified by what other people would think. They kept me hidden."

"How nice," Charlotte said, now blissfully under the spell of his voice.

"They did me no favors," the voice snipped.

The lights in the room grew dimmer. Tobias and Charlotte

could feel panic in their guts, but their minds were so dazed they couldn't stop smiling.

"Can't we just leave?" Tobias struggled to say. "I don't think we belong here."

"You can't leave," the voice replied. "This is your home, and it would be wise for you to stay put. You have been awarded a great gift."

Both kids grinned. The effect of the strange man's voice on their brains was making them feel safe to talk openly.

"Okay," Tobias said.

The lights overhead went out, and the glow behind the mirror grew in intensity. As the glow increased, a dark silhouette behind the glass began to materialize. Tobias and Charlotte squinted and leaned closer. The image coming into view was of a man in a large leather high-back chair. He was old and bald in a way that was both disturbing and unattractive. He sat hunched with his shoulders bending forward. His ears stuck out like fleshy stalks of wheat. His lips were pink and moist, and his nose looked like a small sack of marbles—lumpy and mushed. A large feathery ball was sitting on his bent right shoulder. The ball shivered as the man smiled.

"You're so ugly," Charlotte said kindly.

"I'd be offended if this were the first time I'd heard that," the ugly man said.

Charlotte giggled—she was frightened, but in her state of mind, she couldn't express it correctly.

"My name is Marvin Withers."

Tobias and Charlotte were baffled by the soothing voice that came out of such an ugly mouth.

"Withers like the school?" Tobias asked.

"Yes," Marvin replied. "Like the school."

"Home?" Charlotte blurted.

"This is your home," Marvin informed her. "This has been and always will be. There are worse fates."

Tobias and Charlotte looked at each other. They knew what Marvin was saying was wrong, but for some reason, they both began to clap.

"Very nice," Marvin said. "But it looks like you'll require additional schooling."

The children stopped clapping.

"You like school, remember," Marvin reminded them.

They started to clap again.

"Let me fill you in. You see, my grandparents were the first to climb this mesa. They settled on the top of it and discovered there were things . . . unique to its soil and water—let's just say there's something beneath this mesa that makes people behave in a unique manner."

"There's something beneath this mesa that makes people

behave in a unique manner," both kids chanted as if Marvin had told them to repeat it.

"No," Marvin cooed. "I'm not asking you to mimic my words. I'm telling you things that will help your transition begin. You see, after my grandparents built Witherwood, strange things began to happen. The properties of the soil alone make this ground special. Years later, I was born and it was discovered when I was around seven that my voice could persuade anyone to see things my way. I could even manipulate my parents."

"Dad," Charlotte said, staring blankly.

"Yes," Marvin said. "Both my mom and my dad. When I got older, they tried to tell me how I should act and what I should be. So I used my voice. Tragically, they died following some of my instructions. It's their own fault. Everyone knows that after eating a big meal you should wait twenty minutes before swimming. Especially if you're also unconscious and wearing stone shoes."

Tobias half clapped.

"Thank you," Marvin said sincerely. "Enough history. Now, you've started off on the wrong foot, but there is time to heal the infection you have caused. You will stay away from the second floor. You will forget what you may have seen on the third. You will attend your classes, do your jobs, and cause no more trouble. Treat Witherwood like the institution it is. I believe you will grow to love it here. Understand?"

Tobias and Charlotte nodded so hard it looked like their heads were going to fall off.

"You will forget all that happened tonight. Stick to the places you are instructed to go and eat the food that is placed before you. The food is essential to your change. There is a master plan, and if you are obedient, things will run smoothly. Are we clear?"

"Crystal," Charlotte chirped.

"Good. And you will no longer desire to leave the grounds," Marvin added smoothly.

"Uh-huh," Tobias insisted while nodding.

"I would hate to see what might happen to you two if we were to have another incident like the one you caused earlier," Marvin said sweetly. "You are safe within these walls. We go to great lengths to acquire our students, and it makes me sick thinking about what would happen if you got out. Let's just say that some of the animals that protect Witherwood can't be trusted."

Tobias and Charlotte just stared at him, wishing they could run or scream or, at the very least, stop smiling.

"There is a value to your lives," Marvin practically hummed. "Great worth."

The feathery red ball on his ugly shoulder shook as a round, velvety head rose from the top of it. The head had a beak and a six-inch neck that looked like an empty toilet paper roll. The bird opened its mouth, screeched, and then lowered its head again.

"That's enough for tonight," Marvin said softly. "My voice will stay with you for months before I need to speak to you again. So remember what I have said, and don't forget we're glad you're here."

"Okay," Tobias said cheerily.

The mirror went dark, and the room quietly lit back up. A few moments later, the front door popped open and Orrin entered with the two men. The rash on his arm seemed to have spread to his right cheek, and his limp was more pronounced.

"Did you have a nice talk?" Orrin asked the children.

"Really good," Charlotte replied.

Orrin smiled. "Marvin has such a nice way of saying things. Now, these orderlies will take you to the kitchen."

Tobias and Charlotte were escorted to the kitchen where, for the next four hours, they scrubbed breakfast dishes and helped to prep for lunch. They had missed another night of sleep, but due to the lasting effect of Marvin's voice, they smiled the whole time, all their thoughts and memories of the night no longer in their minds. Charlotte couldn't even remember hating Tobias for the trouble he had put them in.

It was late afternoon when Ms. Gulp finally led them back to their room, door number seven. As usual, there was nobody around. Tobias and Charlotte stared at Ms. Gulp as she motioned for them to go in.

"You're like two strong arguments for youth prison. Go in."

"Thanks," Charlotte said kindly.

"Don't thank me."

Ms. Gulp locked them in their room. Tobias didn't bother turning on the light. He and Charlotte shuffled quickly to their beds and fell facefirst onto their cots.

Neither of them uttered a single word for nearly fifteen hours—unless of course you consider snoring a form of talking.

# CHAPTER 14

# A Little More Learned

*There is something about getting fifteen hours of sleep that makes a previously exhausted person view the world a lot more positively. There is also something sort of painful about fully understanding how bad your situation is because you are now wide awake. And there is the weird way you might feel if someone's voice had altered your mind and made you forget all your troubles.*

Ms. Gulp stepped up to Tobias's cot and put her loud, mushy mouth a few inches away from his right ear. "Morning!"

Tobias's body sprang upward a few inches and then snapped back onto his cot.

"You too, Pointy Ears," she hollered at Charlotte.

Both of them sat up slowly and yawned. They looked at each other and shrugged.

"You'll need to wear these," Ms. Gulp said, throwing a small pile of clothes at both of them. "I'm sick of looking at your filthy rags. You have ten minutes to wash up and change. I'll be waiting in the hall." Ms. Gulp creaked across the floor and left the room.

Tobias gazed at Charlotte and smiled. "I feel different."

"Yeah, me too."

"What happened yesterday?"

Charlotte couldn't remember, so she just yawned again.

Tobias looked at the clothes Ms. Gulp had given him. He held up a small white shirt and a plaid skirt.

"I think those are mine," Charlotte said.

Charlotte used the washroom first. She took a two-minute shower and then put on the plaid skirt, white blouse, kneesocks, and black flats she had been given. She tossed her old clothes into the corner of the bathroom as if she was tossing away hope. She left her blond hair wet and hanging in front of her ears. When she came out, Tobias wanted to laugh, but his head was still foggy.

Tobias took his turn. As he was taking off his clothes, he was happy to find two pens in his pocket, but he was shocked to see all the scratches on his body. He was most surprised by the large red marks on his shoulder. When he combed his hand through the back of his hair, he discovered a clump missing.

"Weird," he said while looking at the mirror.

It took him less than five minutes to shower and change. He then joined his sister and Ms. Gulp in the hall. The uniform Tobias had been given consisted of black corduroy trousers and a collared white shirt with a gray V-neck sweater. There was a red-striped tie included, but he had no idea how to put it on, so he had just thrown it around his neck like a scarf. Seeing this, Ms. Gulp pulled it off of him and began to roughly work it around his neck. Tobias choked as she tightened the knot.

Despite her attempt to strangle him, Tobias said, "Thank you."

Ms. Gulp stared at him with her fat eyes. Her breath smelled like wet garbage, and there were sweat stains showing beneath her armpits. A single long hair was sticking out from her right nostril. "It's obvious Marvin talked to you. Things should run better now."

"You seemed meaner before," Tobias said.

"Watch your tongue," Ms. Gulp warned, her red hair pinned back so tightly that her face looked like a blotchy plastic mask. "I'm exactly the same person. Now, come with me, or you'll be late."

All three of them walked through Weary Hall to the arched

doors leading out into the gardens. Outside it was raining, and the trees and bushes hung their branches, seeming depressed about the weather.

Tobias glanced around as they trudged down the stone corridor that ran alongside the gardens.

"Were we here last night?" he asked, confused.

"Don't ask me that," Ms. Gulp barked as she marched two paces ahead of them. "I detest inquisitive children. What good can come of a child's question?"

Tobias tried asking Charlotte. "Were we here last night?"

"Don't ask her questions either," Ms. Gulp snipped.

Charlotte looked at her brother and shrugged.

They entered Severe Hall.

"Just so you don't ask me later, Severe Hall is where most of the schoolrooms are," Ms. Gulp said. "It's time for you to make something of yourselves—you know . . . give to the cause."

It's important to point out that some words seem to have impact beyond their consonants and vowels. Yes, sinister inflection can turn harmless little letters into statements of dread and uneasiness. Had the Eggers kids been clear minded, they would have turned and run because of the way Ms. Gulp had said "give to the cause." But their minds were still covered in the goo of Marvin's voice, so Charlotte said, "That sounds fun."

Inside Severe Hall, the walls were paneled with dark wood that ran from floor to ceiling. The windows were filled with textured glass that allowed light through in thin yellow streaks. There were tree-shaped chandeliers hanging from dusty black chains. And a large painting on the wall showed the image of a child riding a lion. At the end of the hall was a single door with a small plaque that read LEARNING ANNEX.

Ms. Gulp opened the door. "Go in."

Tobias and Charlotte stepped into the classroom, followed by Ms. Gulp. Dozens of desks filled the room, and dozens of students filled the desks. Everyone turned to stare. The other students were dressed in the same uniforms. There looked to be an even number of girls and boys.

The walls in the classroom were covered with fuzzy brown burlap that muffled any noise in the room. Two plants hung in the far corners, their long branches spilling out of their pots and touching the floor like leafy octopi.

In the front of the classroom, there was a man leaning on the edge of an old desk. Behind him was a wall-sized chalkboard with sketches of various animals and numbers on it. The man's arms and legs were as thin as twigs, and his head was sharp and covered with scruffy bark-colored hair. He was obviously the teacher, but he didn't look as ancient as the rest of the Witherwood staff. He had a quick smile that he displayed the second Tobias and Charlotte entered.

"Come, come." He waved. "You must be the new students I keep hearing about. Have a seat here in the front."

The teacher pointed to a couple of empty desks in the front row. Tobias and Charlotte shuffled over to them.

"They're spirited, so teach them quickly," Ms. Gulp said. "Orrin wants them on the fast track. Time matters with these two."

"I'll have them ready," the teacher assured her. "Up to speed ASAP."

Ms. Gulp slammed the door behind her, causing every student in the room to jump.

"Introductions are in order," the teacher said in a soft voice. "I'm Professor Jacob Himzakity. If it helps, you can remember it by thinking about someone pointing at me and saying, 'Him's a kitty.' Understand?"

Tobias kind of nodded, but Charlotte just stared at him.

"And your names?" he asked.

"I'm Tobias, and she's Charlotte."

"Well, Tobias and Charlotte, this is adaptation class. You will be brought here every day by Ms. Gulp until I feel you are ready to come on your own. Okay?"

Neither one of them nodded.

"I will teach you what you need to know. Deal?"

"Yes," Charlotte said, her ears twitching slightly.

Tobias thought about saying yes as well, but for some reason his brain was acting up, and something wasn't connecting right. Maybe it was the years of being mischievous, or the fact that he had never taken instruction well and now he was getting way too much of it. Maybe it was the déjà-vu–like feelings he was having, the memories of the gardens and of things that may or may not have happened there. Or perhaps it was the odd scratches and bruises he had on his body. Whatever it was, it wasn't sitting well with his brain.

"And you?" Professor Himzakity asked Tobias. "Will you be respectful so I can shape your mind?"

Tobias nodded.

"Fantastic!"

Tobias and Charlotte slowly looked around the room. Right behind them was a large boy with dark skin and no hair. Next to him were two girls who were obviously twins—both had long brown hair and stout pale noses. There were too many other sets of eyes and faces to take in. All the students were quiet, and only the bald-headed boy acknowledged them by giving a slight nod.

"Now," Professor Himzakity said, "I know it's hard to stay focused with the parade just days away, but we've much to learn and only ... well ... only your youth to learn it in." He pulled open one of his desk drawers and withdrew a textbook. He walked over to Tobias's desk and slapped it down. "You'll need to share with your sister."

Tobias stared at the front of the book. The cover was a collage of different animal pictures. In one top corner was a picture of a frog. The image jogged something in Tobias's mind, and he spoke without thinking,

"Tadpoles."

"Yes, yes," Professor Himzakity said happily. "We will study the frog and its adaptive properties starting next month. For now, however, we are thinking about insects."

Tobias looked at his smiling sister and begged his mind to kick in. He felt contented, but he knew he shouldn't. He scooted his desk a little bit closer to Charlotte's so they could share the book.

Professor Himzakity talked fast and repeated the same facts over and over. "Crickets can hear using their legs. Crickets can hear using their legs..." The professor then made all the students chant what he had said back at him.

After three hours of this unusual recitation, a couple of attendants wheeled in a lunch cart. The cart was filled with food—sandwiches, chocolate pudding, and drinks. One of the attendants clapped, and the students got up and began to pick what they wanted from the cart. Everyone was given two mandatory servings of pudding. Tobias was surprised to notice that his food had no smell. It hardly had any taste as well.

The bald boy looked up from his food and smiled at Tobias. "I'm Archie."

Tobias and Charlotte nodded in acknowledgment.

"People say I'm friendly, but I can't always remember if I am."

"You are," Charlotte said.

"I must have learned that growing up," Archie said proudly.

"Where'd you grow up?" Tobias asked.

Archie tilted his head and scrunched his forehead. "What do you mean?"

"I mean where are you from?"

"I can't really remember."

"Maybe he was born at school?" Charlotte joined in.

"Maybe," Archie said. "I can't remember being anywhere else. Where are you from?"

"I'm not sure," Tobias answered in a confused tone. "Michigan?"

"That doesn't sound right," Charlotte said.

"It probably isn't," Tobias admitted. "I guess I can't remember either."

A few more students gathered around Tobias and Charlotte and began to point at Charlotte's ears and ask them meaningless questions. The Eggers kids tried their best to answer, but their brains were failing them.

When there was a break in the interrogation, Tobias decided to ask a question himself. "What's Student Morale Day?"

"Just one of the best days of the year," Archie answered for everyone. "The teachers put on an amazing parade, and you get to clap and wave as much as you want. Two years ago, Professor Himzakity tossed out mints from his parade float."

"Sounds great," Charlotte said.

"It was. In fact, people are still talking about it. I know I am." Archie smiled. "Witherwood really is a wonderful place. You two are lucky to be here."

"We know that," Charlotte said.

A bell sounded, and the students shuffled back to their seats. Archie looked at Tobias and smiled. Professor Himzakity called the class to order as the attendants took the cart and left.

"Well," the professor said smugly, "I hope you enjoyed the food we provided you."

Charlotte nodded, while Tobias stared at the cover of his book, begging his brain to hurry up and kick in.

Professor Himzakity looked at Tobias and Charlotte. "Why don't you two scoot your desks even closer?" he suggested. "It will be easier for you to focus on the book."

Tobias grabbed the edge of his desk and jerked it toward Charlotte's. Charlotte, thinking it was her responsibility to move closer to him, jerked hers toward him at the same time. As a result, her desk jammed directly into Tobias's fingers. It was the kind of hit that would make even the toughest person wince—like stubbing your toe hard against a metal table leg on a very cold night and then taking a whack at it with a sledgehammer. The sharp bolt of pain shot through Tobias's arm and up to his brain.

Tobias leapt from his desk, screaming and waving his hand. Professor Himzakity put both of his hands on his cheeks and howled like a sympathetic stick. Everyone else just watched Tobias's embarrassing dance and tried not to laugh.

After about thirty seconds, Tobias settled down and slipped back into his chair.

"Sorry," Charlotte said.

Tobias wanted to holler a bit more, but there was something about the horrific, shocking pain that had cleared a small portion of his head. He shook his wounded fingers and stared at his sister.

"Don't worry about it," he finally said.

Professor Himzakity stepped over and looked at Tobias's fingers. "They don't appear to be broken," he said. "You'll have some tremendous swelling."

Tobias kept quiet as his fingers throbbed.

Professor Himzakity walked back to the front and began to

lecture about the need for obedience and how the world had forgotten its importance.

It struck a partially clear-minded Tobias that what his professor was now teaching didn't seem to have much to do with animals.

## CHAPTER 15

# A TAXI DRIVER NAMED SAM

*Sometimes the things we don't understand are frightening. I don't understand algebra as much as I should. That's why I would hate to run into algebra in a dark alley. Tobias had been in a happy, foggy state, but now his brain was reminding him that there were a lot of things at Witherwood he didn't understand. Strangely, he couldn't decide whether he should be happy or terrified.*

Ralph Eggers looked out the taxi's window, desperately searching for any sign of something he might remember. Life had been very strenuous the last couple of days as he had come to grips with not knowing who he was. It was hard to function when you couldn't remember your own name. You and I might know he's Ralph Eggers, but he surely did not.

Physically, Ralph was in good shape, aside from the broken arm and a few small cuts. After the doctor had discovered Ralph's amnesia, the hospital had kept him an additional three days for testing. What they learned was that Ralph had lost all of his personal memories. He could remember how to eat, but he couldn't remember a single meal he had ever eaten. Likewise, he knew there were fifty states, but he couldn't remember if he had ever visited any of them. He was perfectly healthy, but he was missing his memories.

The hospital checked with the police to see if there were any missing persons, but none had been reported. So needing the bed space, they had discharged Ralph. Having nowhere else to go, he headed to the local YMCA to live until he figured out who he was or until somebody came looking for him.

Mr. Eggers checked into the YMCA and immediately called a taxi. The Red Cross had given him a few hundred dollars before he left the hospital to help him get back on his feet. So Ralph used some of that money to pay for the taxi he was now riding in.

The taxi driver was a medium-sized fellow with a big belly. He had wiry black hair that was thinning unevenly on the top. His eyes were close together, and his nose was smashed over to the right side. His taxi smelled like beef jerky and bubble gum. Ralph had chosen to sit up in the passenger seat so he wouldn't feel like he was being chauffeured.

"And you don't even know your name?" the taxi driver asked in amazement as they drove along the freeway through the desolate outskirts of town.

"No," Ralph said sadly. "One of the nurses called me Blank, because I'm sort of like a blank piece of paper."

"Blank's not the worst name," the taxi driver said. "I got a cousin named Stunk."

"Really? I guess I should be happy with Blank, then. What's your name?"

"Sam. Pretty boring, I know. So you don't remember anything?"

Ralph nodded.

"No fooling? And you aren't just pretending to avoid paying some bills or to get away from someone who's after you?"

"I don't think so."

"How'd you break that arm?"

"I don't know. I can't remember anything."

"Then where are we going?"

"The doctor gave me the name of the rancher who found me. I thought I'd talk to him first."

"You think he'll know something?"

"Maybe. There has to be a reason I was wandering out here. I mean, look at this place. There's nothing."

"Yep, it's a lonely desert. I don't know why anyone would

come out here. But it's gonna cost you. This isn't exactly a short drive, and gas ain't free these days."

"I know," Ralph said.

"No memory at all," Sam said, whistling. "That's something. What about a wife or kids?"

"Not sure. I wasn't wearing a wedding ring when they found me."

"Maybe you were trying to get away from something," Sam said, playing detective. "Maybe you were running from the law."

"I don't feel like a criminal."

"Nah." Sam waved one hand dismissively. "And you don't look like one. Course, my cousin Stunk looks pretty clean, and he's no good."

"Sorry to hear that."

"Yeah, so's his mother," Sam added. "I'm not sure there's much hope for Stunk, but it'll be interesting to see if this rancher has some answers for you."

Ralph nodded.

"It's kinda like you were adopted and we're trying to find where you came from," Sam said.

"I guess you're right."

"You and I are sort of alike. You have no ties that you know of, and neither do I. I drive this taxi because I don't want anyone telling me what to do. I can work as much or as little as I please, and I have no wife and children to go home to."

"I guess that's good," Ralph said skeptically.

"I don't know. Maybe it ain't that great."

"Yeah," Ralph agreed.

Sam pressed on the gas pedal and headed down the freeway toward the address Ralph had given him, 2527 Battered Cactus Road.

# CHAPTER 16

# STUDENT MORALE DAY

*There's nothing very amazing about doing the same thing over and over. Not many people in the world are satisfied with performing the same tasks all day—every day. Even great things grow boring if repeated too often. Swinging can be fun, but if you're forced to swing for eight hours of the day, it gets old. It's the same thing with eating. Most people enjoy a good meal, but if you were commanded to eat all day, you would not only get bored, you'd get sick and fat.*

Well, for the next few days, Tobias and Charlotte had to do the same thing over and over. And unfortunately for them, they didn't have the luxury of doing something that was fun. Nope, their days started out awful and stayed that way. But today was different. It was Friday. It had been a full week since their father had dropped them off, and already they were beginning to grow familiar with their surroundings. Today was also the much-talked-about Student Morale Day. Witherwood was buzzing.

Professor Himzakity wanted his class to have good seats for the parade, so he had let them eat their lunches outdoors. They had set their chairs up along the one wide path that ran diagonally through the northwest corner of the gardens. Other students brought out chairs and were taking their places for the festivities as well. As usual, everyone was served sandwiches, apples, and endless chocolate pudding. The weather was warm, and the sky was filled with clouds. There was something magical and comforting about the gardens during the day, and at the moment, things felt even more interesting.

"It feels like I'm dreaming," Charlotte said. "I think I love it here."

Tobias didn't feel the same. He wanted to tell Charlotte that any dreams she was having were really nightmares, but he held his tongue. He would have been just as blindly happy had he not been jolted out of it by the painful smack to his hand from the desks. His mind was clear. It was obvious to him that it was not only Charlotte who had been brainwashed by Marvin, but all of the other students as well. None of them knew where they had come from or how long they had been at Witherwood, and no-body seemed to care. In fact, they all seemed happy.

"It's so nice out," Charlotte said. "And a parade for us. How great."

"Yeah," Tobias agreed, looking up at a long banner that said STUDENT MORALE DAY hanging from one of the lampposts. He studied the gardens around them, curious as to where all the animals they had been chased by were. He thought about Lars, the small creature they had found, and wondered if he had survived.

"I like the gardens," Charlotte said.

Tobias wanted to holler and tell everyone what was going on, but for the time being, he needed to act dumb so that nobody would take him to Marvin again. He needed time to figure out a solution to their bleak situation.

In the last two days, he had been working hard to map out every bit of Witherwood he had seen and could remember. He had taken some paper from the trash in the kitchen and used his pens. He had drawn their room, the second floor, the gardens, the halls, the kitchen and cellar, and of course the square room. He hid the papers under the loose floorboard in his room. As his mind got clearer, he kept remembering more and more things to document and map.

At night when Charlotte was asleep, Tobias explored

Witherwood, carefully avoiding the singing voices that roamed the halls. He had made a new key from another old spring, and it worked well. Last night he had discovered a library in Severe Hall that he was hoping to get back to explore tonight.

"Eat your pudding," one of the teachers said through a megaphone. "The parade will begin shortly."

As they all ate, sunshine slid down through the tall cottonwoods in the gardens and painted the students' faces with shadows and light. It made Tobias look illuminated and caused Charlotte's white skin to appear cracked and uneven. Archie was sitting next to Charlotte. He leaned over to ask if she wanted to trade him her sandwich for his apple.

"They won't give me a fourth sandwich," he complained.

Charlotte smiled and made the trade.

Archie's bald head reflected some of the light from above. His brown skin and dark green eyes made him look wise. However, the things he said often made him sound the opposite. He took a big bite, chewed a little, and then looked at Tobias and said, "I'm glad you guys are here."

"Really?" Tobias asked. "Why?"

"Because she shares," Archie said, holding up the sandwich.

Charlotte stared at him. "Where's your hair?" she asked. "You're not old. You should have hair."

"I don't know where it went. I used to have a lot, and then one morning I woke up and it was gone. I was sad at first, but now I don't mind. Being bald is sort of my thing."

"Did you go to the doctor?" Tobias asked.

"No. Ms. Gulp took a look at it. She said it's fine."

A small band of teachers began to play music on trumpets and drums, announcing that the parade was about to start.

"Don't you think there's something unusual about this school?" Tobias asked, desperately wanting to know more about what was going on here. "Something mysterious?"

"It's just a school," Archie said, confused. "But there is a secret."

Tobias leaned in over Charlotte and closer to Archie.

"I shouldn't talk about it," Archie uttered guiltily. "But the Catchers are real."

"Catchers?" Tobias asked, his heart pounding.

"Quiet," Archie said, suddenly nervous. "Or you'll lose your hair too."

"What are they?"

"I can't remember. Sometimes I hear things, and I'm not sure what to do about it. I also don't know where the older kids go."

"What older kids?" Tobias asked. "Do people graduate? Do they get out?"

"I can't talk about this anymore," Archie said sadly. "The parade's going to start."

"But—" Tobias tried.

"Parade," Archie insisted.

Large wood doors in the middle of Never Hall were pulled open, and the band began to play louder. Everyone's head turned to see what was coming through the doors. A cart with wooden wheels was being pulled by two teachers. It was the first float in the parade. In honor of Student Morale Day, all the teachers were wearing colorful suits and ties. On top of the first wagon was a miniature replica of the mesa with a little model of Witherwood. Painted on the side of the wagon in blue were the words STU-DENT MORALE DAY.

"Everyone clap!" one of the teachers near them ordered.

All the students surrounding Tobias and Charlotte began to clap excitedly. The first float passed slowly in front of them, moving down the wide dirt path. Right behind the first entry, there was another large wagon being pulled by Orrin and a tall woman. Orrin had on a faded tan suit that made him look like a short ice cream cone with a scoop of bald on the top. Their float was a papier-mâché man that had no facial features and was missing his left hand. The word painted on the wagon said CHARACTER. Tobias watched students he didn't know on the other side of the path clapping and waving madly.

"Is it just me, or are these floats lame?"

"It's just you," Charlotte said. "Look how beautiful."

Charlotte was pointing to the third float, which was a faded papier-mâché rock with the word COMMITMENT painted on it.

"Really?" Tobias said.

Charlotte clapped even harder.

Professor Himzakity was pulling the fourth float with another male teacher. The professor waved as much as he could while he pulled. His sticklike body was dressed in a green suit and a pink tie. In the outfit he resembled a praying mantis. He pulled with one hand and waved at his students with the other. Everyone waved back with vigor. As he passed by, he reached into his pocket and pulled out a handful of Life Savers. He threw them, and the students went wild.

"They're going to be talking about this for years!" Archie said, holding on to a Life Saver he had caught and looking like he was about to cry.

On the float Professor Himzakity was pulling, there was a big pot with a short teacher standing in it. The teacher had a megaphone and kept repeating, "Established in 1805, established in 1805 . . ."

The noise of the megaphone and the small band combined with the clapping of the students to make a sound that almost resembled fun. A wagon with the word SCIENCE on the side and a papier-mâché rainbow on top passed by, followed by a wagon being pulled by Ms. Gulp. She was wearing a gold suit that was a bit too tight. It was weird to see her in pants. Her float had two cardboard boxes covered with paper flowers. Painted on the side were the words PROPER BEHAVIOR.

"I've never seen anything like this," Tobias said in disgust. "This is what they were bragging about."

"I know," Charlotte said. "I wish it would never end."

Well, it did. There was just one more float, and it was the most surprising. Sitting on top of a wooden wagon was Fiddle. He was in a big leather chair holding his Rubik's Cube and staring out at the other students. He looked lost and confused. Painted on the wagon was the word WITHERS.

Tobias tried to get Fiddle's attention, but he was engrossed in his cube and trying not to look up.

"Fiddle!"

The crowd was so loud Tobias could hardly hear himself. As soon as Fiddle's float passed, the band started playing faster, and all the carts turned around and headed back through the large wood doors. As quickly as it had begun, the parade was over.

Tobias looked around. "That was it?"

"Best one yet," Archie said as he sucked on his Life Saver. "I can't wait until the next."

"I agree," Charlotte said.

Students began to pick up their chairs to carry inside as

teachers ordered some of the more enthusiastic kids to stop waving. Charlotte complained about still being hungry, so Tobias tore the remainder of his sandwich in half and gave part to her. The smell from the ripped sandwich was strong. Ever since his brain had cleared, Tobias could smell better than ever. He breathed in, trying to pinpoint what the mysterious ingredient was as Charlotte ate.

"Ready?" he asked.

Charlotte smiled. "So do you think they'll finally give us pillows tonight?"

Tobias shook his head and shoved the rest of his sandwich in his mouth. He stared at Archie as he stood up and grabbed his chair.

"So what else do you know about the Catchers?"

"What?" Archie asked, confused.

Tobias didn't have the energy to keep going round. The parade was over, and Archie was done talking.

After school, Tobias and Charlotte worked four hours in the kitchen and then Ms. Gulp took them to their room. Charlotte walked straight to her pillowless cot and went to bed.

Tobias did not. Student Morale Day had been a disappointment, and he was hoping tonight would be different.

# CHAPTER 17

# LIBRARIES ARE NOT STORAGE LOCKERS

Tobias Eggers was becoming much more than just a scared boy trapped in an unusual school. Now he was more like a brave boy temporarily detained in a place he was secretly mapping and slowly figuring out. He really wanted to see what they were hiding on the third floor. He couldn't remember exactly what he had seen through that third-story window, but he knew it had made him uneasy.

Tobias focused on what he wanted to accomplish tonight. He had a goal. He was going to visit the library he had found and see if it held any answers to Witherwood's secrets. He was also going to be on the lookout for anything that mentioned the word *Catchers*.

Ever since talking to Archie, there had been little else Tobias could think of. He knew there was something important about the Catchers and their relationship to Witherwood.

As Charlotte lay there sleeping, Tobias couldn't help but notice how much older she seemed. It had been just over a week, yet it felt like a lifetime had passed and that his sister was no longer the kid she had been when they stood at the iron gate and wondered what would happen next.

Tobias got up from his cot and walked to the corner where the loose floorboard was. He pulled it back and took out his paper and pen. He drew the parts of the gardens he had seen today. He drew Professor Himzakity and wrote small notes about him around the edge. Things that he might want to remember if he was ever a victim of Marvin's voice again. He wrote down some of the odd things that the professor had them repeat: "Once a person lets go of something, it's no longer theirs" and "Youth belongs to those who have fortune."

After Tobias had written and drawn what he needed, he put the papers back and placed the board over them. He then slid beneath his cot and wrote a couple of notes to himself on the underside. He had been carefully placing clues all over that would help him remember things if he ever had his brain messed with again. If he lost his mind, he at least wanted a fighting chance to get it back.

Tobias scooted out from under the cot and stood up. Brushing his hands together, he walked to the door and took out his key. He slid it into the old keyhole, and the lock tumbled open. He listened for voices, but there was no sound of singing.

Carefully, he made his way through Weary Hall and over to Severe Hall with the help of tiny yellow lights lining the walls. Witherwood felt warm, like an oven that had retained its heat after baking a large meal. He wasn't wearing his school sweater, but he rolled up his shirtsleeves in an effort to cool down.

Near the middle of Severe Hall, there were doors that opened onto a spacious foyer lit only by a single lamp on the far wall. On the other side of the foyer, there was an archway with wide wood doors that were locked. A gold plaque to the side of the arch read LIBRARY.

The air in the foyer was quiet and filled with the smell of dirt. Tobias's nose let him know that someone had left an apple in the bottom of a small trash bin beneath a stone table.

While exploring last night, Tobias had discovered that his key worked for the library. He unlocked it and pushed the right-side door open just slightly. He slipped in and relocked the door. A dozen square windows on both sides of the building let in enough moonlight for Tobias to see. The library was enormous, with tall ceilings that were easily as high as the third floor. Bookshelves filled the walls, and every shelf was stuffed with books. Rows of wooden desks littered the floor, and the round table in the middle of the room looked like a gaping mouth. There were chairs all over and tables with boxes stacked on top of them. The boxes made the library look more like a storage room than a place of learning.

Tobias didn't know where to start. He wanted to find answers, but he wasn't even sure what questions he had. He wished Charlotte were with him so they could split the work. But Charlotte was sleeping, and he was all he had at the moment. So he wandered the rows of books and climbed the rolling ladders to high shelves, looking for anything that might appear to be an answer. Dust and feathery cobwebs were everywhere; no one had used the library in a while.

Tobias looked under *W* for *Witherwood*. There was nothing. A book titled *Hyrum Withers: Man of Science and the Supernatural* caught his attention, but it was long, and the words were little, and it would have taken him two months to read it. So he flipped to the index in the back and looked up *Catchers*. There was just one reference, page 452. Tobias read the one line that mentioned them: "The Catchers are essential to our prosperity. They are the silent hands of Witherwood."

There was nothing else.

"What is this place?" he whispered to himself. "What school needs silent hands?"

Tobias shut the book and shelved it. He looked for books on Catchers, but there weren't any in the *C* section. He even tried looking in the *T* section for *the Catchers*, but that was pretty much a pointless endeavor from the start. As he was looking in the *K* section in case someone had accidentally spelled *Catcher* with a *K*, he heard what sounded like a key slide into the lock. Tobias slipped behind the shelf and held his breath. The library door opened, and overhead lights snapped on. There was the sound of footsteps and now the smell of old person was in the air.

Over the books and through the bookshelves, he could see Orrin and Professor Himzakity.

"We are on schedule as always," Himzakity said. "The Gothiks will be stocked, and the demand is higher than ever."

"Good news indeed," Orrin replied. "This will be a profitable spring for Witherwood."

Tobias turned his right ear to better hear.

"This library is a cemetery," Professor Himzakity said. "A storage room with books. We could use this space for so much more."

"Be careful what you say about libraries," Orrin scolded. "There's much to fear and favor about books."

"And much to forget," Professor Himzakity snipped.

"Let's not have words," Orrin said. "It's a pleasant night, and tomorrow we begin this semester's extractions."

The word *extractions* made Tobias lose his breath. He shifted uncomfortably behind the shelf. The dust in the library was making his nose drip wildly, so he held one of his fingers up to his nose to keep from sneezing. As he lifted his arm, his elbow knocked the shelf, causing an almost inaudible thump.

"Wait," Orrin said. "Did you hear something?"

Tobias held his breath.

"Stay here," Orrin whispered.

Through the books, Tobias could see Orrin coming closer. Moving like a crab, he scurried backward until he met up with the far library wall, near the books about earth science. He couldn't see Orrin any longer, but he could hear his uneven footsteps getting closer. Tobias looked around frantically. He reached for a thick book on the bottom shelf where he was crouching. His plan was to defend himself with the volume, but when he pulled it out, he saw a knob on the wall behind where the book had been. Tobias reached back into the shelf and pushed the knob. The three bottom bookshelves slid quietly to the right, exposing a small opening into a long, dark space.

Orrin was getting closer.

Having no other option, Tobias crawled into the opening and hit the knob again. The shelves slid back into place, leaving him in the dark and behind the wall. He stood up and held his breath. A tiny sliver of light shone through the crack at the bottom of the moving shelves. He could hear Orrin as he slowly passed the shelf. Orrin stopped and scratched his arms.

"Come on," Professor Himzakity called. "Get your book. We need to prepare."

"I'm coming. I think my ears need a cleaning."

Orrin's footsteps faded, and a few moments later the sliver of light flicked off. Tobias was alone, in the dark, behind the wall.

"What now?" he whispered to himself.

Instead of going back out into the library, he decided to turn and travel farther into the unknown passageway. It was black, but the possibility of where it might lead was too tempting to ignore.

"It has to lead out," he said, trying to psych himself up.

Tobias stood and walked cautiously behind the walls.

# CHAPTER 18

# A Small Mention of Something Important

It was dark by the time Ralph Eggers and his taxi driver, Sam, found 2527 Battered Cactus Road. It was located in the center of nowhere on a section of dirt in the middle of vast fields of cattle and crops. Ralph rang the doorbell and stood on the doorstep with Sam.

A squatty woman in jeans and a pink blouse opened the door. She had suspicious eyes and a tight smile.

"Yes?" she asked.

"Hello," Ralph said, looking at the slip of paper in his hand. "Is Donald Tilt in?"

"He's out on the far edge of the ranch."

"Can we wait?" Ralph asked. "I'm the person he found walking around last week. I was hoping I could ask him a few questions."

"It's nice to see you're okay," the woman said. "Well, you're welcome to come in and wait, but it could be some time before Mr. Tilt returns."

Ralph looked at Sam. "Can we wait?"

"I suppose," Sam said.

The woman ushered them into a large room with vaulted ceilings and a mammoth fireplace in the middle. The walls were covered with mounted animal heads, and the floor displayed animal skins. Most of the dead animals were familiar, but a few had the look of being strange and exotic. The ceiling was made of thick wood beams, and there was a full-sized stuffed bear standing in the center of the room. The smell of burning wood filled the air.

"I don't like this room," Sam whispered.

The woman brought them a couple of drinks and a tray full of cheese and meat.

"I guess it could grow on me," Sam added as he sat down and did his best to empty the tray.

It was a good while before Donald Tilt finally returned. He was a tall man with wide shoulders and a long waist. His hands were as big as mitts, and he had a short beard that covered most of his thin face. He introduced himself and then ran off to wash up. Half an hour later, he emerged from his bedroom wearing a worn blue sports coat, dark jeans, and boots that had a large *D* and a large *T* burnt into the side of them. Donald poured himself a cup of coffee and then took a seat on one of the leather couches.

"I see you've met some of my friends," Donald said, motioning to the animals on the walls.

"You shoot your friends?" Sam asked with concern.

"Shoot 'em and eat 'em," Donald answered in a friendly tone. "Hunting is a big part of my life."

"I just think—" Sam started to protest, but Ralph stopped him by holding his right palm up.

"What Sam is trying to say is thanks for taking the time to talk to me."

"My pleasure," Donald said, unfazed by Sam's protest. "I must say, you look a lot different than when I last saw you. For one thing, you're dressed."

Ralph's face reddened. "About that, I was hoping you might know more as to why I was out there."

"I wish I did, but I'm sorry to say there's not much more I can tell you. I told the doctors everything. I was out checking on the herd in the far part of my property, there by the interstate. I had just gotten out of my truck and was walking over to the new fences when you came up. You kinda spooked me 'cause you weren't wearing much, and your body was covered with dust so you sort of blended into the dirt. In fact, you might think I'm crazy, but for a split second when I first saw you, I thought you were a ghost."

"Probably the ghost of one of these animals you shot," Sam said.

"Who are you?" Donald asked Sam nicely.

"I'm his taxi driver," Sam answered. "And I'm not too crazy about hunters."

"Well, Sam," Donald said kindly, "I figure there're a number of critters that would love to come back and haunt me. But it wasn't one of them. It was him." Donald pointed at Ralph and smiled.

"What happened then?" Ralph asked.

"Like I told the doc, you were babbling and sort of tearing at your skin as if you were hot. It was a terribly warm day, and you drank about a gallon of water. I asked you your name, and all you said was *Martha*."

"Martha?" Ralph asked, surprised. "Nobody told me that."

"Well, whether someone told you or not, it's true," Donald said. "You said *Martha* and then just went on babbling. I asked you if you'd like a ride into town, and you climbed in my car without saying another word. I drove you straight to the hospital, dropped you off, and then had a meal in the hospital's cafeteria. I wouldn't recommend the meat loaf."

"Thanks," Ralph said. "So did I say anything as you were driving?"

"Not really," Donald replied. "You kept turning on the radio because you thought it was the heater. And you rolled your window down once."

Ralph was silent in thought.

"I wish I could tell you more," Donald said sympathetically. "I truly do, but that's all that happened."

"Can you think of any reason I'd be out there?"

"Not really," Donald answered, stroking his beard with his hand. "It's pretty desolate. I wondered if you might be some sort of nature freak wanting to be one with the world."

"I don't think that's it."

"No, I don't think so either," Donald agreed. "But there's nothing out there aside from empty land and a hundred head of cattle."

"Nothing else?" Ralph said.

"Well, there's the river near the old highway and the abandoned rest stop, but nobody travels down that road any longer. The only thing that way is Witherwood." Donald shivered.

"Who's Witherwood?" Sam questioned.

"Not a who, but a what," Donald said uneasily. "It's some sort of school on top of the mesa. It's been there forever. I grew up with my parents telling me ghost stories about it. It scared the muck out of me then and still gives me the chills. It's not a good place."

"Witherwood," Ralph said slowly. "Maybe I wandered off from there."

"Does it ring a bell?" Sam asked.

"No," Ralph replied. "So how do we get there?"

"You go back to the interstate and head south," Donald explained. "Get off at the ranch road exit, stay to the left, and travel down the old highway. Eventually there will be a road on your right. I can't remember the name of it, but it's the only road. If you pass the abandoned rest stop, you've gone too far. Take that road up to the school. It's a steep drive to the top of the mesa, but eventually you'll reach Witherwood. It's not a place you want to visit at night."

"It can't be that bad," Ralph said.

"It is or it isn't," Donald replied. "I've heard people say it's a place of great scientific learning, and it's only for the most gifted kids, but there are also some nuts who think it's haunted."

"Really?" Ralph asked. "And you believe that?"

"Whether I do or don't, I'd still stay away from that road at night."

"So we'll come back in the morning," Sam said. "I'm not driving around here at night, especially when there are people who might shoot me."

"I can't afford to pay you to drive me back tomorrow," Ralph said anxiously. "Maybe we should just go tonight."

"I've got news for you—you can't afford to even pay me for all of today," Sam replied. "But that's okay, I wanna see what happens. Of course I prefer to see what happens in the daytime."

"I'll tell you boys what," Donald said, standing up. "I know it's late, but I haven't eaten. So if you wanna join me, I'll have my staff cook us some steaks and you can sleep in one of our guest rooms."

"Really?" Ralph asked, surprised by Donald's generosity.

"I won't take no for an answer."

"What do you say, Sam?" Ralph asked.

"I've got nothing to drive home to," Sam replied. "But are the guest rooms filled with more of these animals? Because I'm not sure I could sleep."

"You're one heck of a taxi driver," Donald said, laughing.

"Ain't that the truth," Sam agreed.

Donald laughed, then picked up a bell sitting on a table and rang it.

CHAPTER 19

# WINDOW OF OPPORTUNITY

*We all have things to do. Most of us need to take out the trash, or empty the dishwasher, or brush our teeth. Some of us need to get to work; a few of us probably have homework; and there are some out there who simply need to get a move on, whatever that means. Our lives are filled with tasks and projects. Today might be the day you need to fix that gate. Or maybe there's a puzzle that has been put away and needs to be pieced together. Now might be a good time to get that puzzle out, put it together, and discover that the finished picture is actually a map that will lead you to great riches—riches so extraordinary that from this point on, you can lie in a hammock and do nothing for the rest of your days.*

**S**ee? We all have things to do.

Well, Tobias had been doing something. He had gotten to the library, gotten away from Orrin, and found a secret space behind the walls. The space was thin and dark, but Tobias could stand and walk. He held his hand out in front and shuffled his feet forward to feel for anything that might stop or harm him. The passageway seemed to go only in one direction. After a bend, it ran for a long distance and then bent again. Tobias tried to remember each shuffle and step so he could record it. Just past the second bend, it came to a stop. He pushed a latch and was surprised to step out through one of the tall storage lockers near the corner of Weary Hall. Tobias had hoped the passage might lead him outside, but it seemed to just be a connection between an old locker and an unused library.

He closed the locker, noted its number, and made it back to his room without incident. It was past ten, and he was wrestling with himself over going to sleep or trying to make an escape now. Sleep sounded wonderful, but freedom sounded better. He probably would have gone with sleeping if it had not been for what he had overheard Orrin say: "Tomorrow we will begin this semester's extractions."

Tobias didn't know what Orrin meant, but he had no desire to be extracted.

Inside his room he quickly took out his papers and added the details of the library and hidden passage to his map. He scribbled the word *Gothiks*. Something about the way Orrin had said it made it feel important. After returning the paper to its spot under the floorboard, he walked over to Charlotte. She was in a dead sleep, making him feel almost bad about what he was about to do—almost.

The time had come to inflict a little pain and see if he could get his sister's mind back.

Kneeling next to her bed, he reached out and put one hand on her right shoulder and his other hand over her mouth. Tobias took a deep breath and began to shake her.

Charlotte's brown eyes flashed open, and she tried to scream.

"Quiet," Tobias whispered. "You need to be quiet."

"Mffrllllfruup," she said from beneath his hand.

"If I take it off, you have to be quiet," Tobias insisted.

Charlotte nodded, and Tobias removed his hand.

"I was sleeping!"

"I know," Tobias replied. "That's why I woke you. You have to get up—we're leaving."

Charlotte tried to close her eyes, but Tobias wouldn't stand for it.

"Listen to me. Do you want to just keep doing this forever?

Reciting things for hours, doing dishes, and sleeping—that's not a life."

"It's fine, and I like the sleeping part," Charlotte insisted.

"This isn't sleeping," Tobias argued. "We don't even have pillows. You're just so exhausted you don't care."

"Okay," Charlotte slurred.

"I didn't want to do this, but it worked for me."

"You don't want to do—"

Tobias grabbed a tiny bit of the back of Charlotte's upper arm and pinched, while twisting it as hard as he possibly could. It was a move Charlotte herself used to use on him whenever they fought. Now he was doing it in hopes of shocking her back into reality. He tried to remember all the times his sister had been mean to him in hopes of making himself feel better about hurting her.

He put his other hand over Charlotte's mouth as she screamed. She sat up and swung her legs over the edge of the cot. When her feet hit the floor, Tobias lifted his right leg and slammed his foot down as hard as he could on her toes. He placed both his hands over her mouth as she drew in breath to scream even louder.

"Shhhh," Tobias begged. "You have to keep quiet."

Charlotte sobbed and bit at Tobias's hands, but he kept them in place and smothered her screams. It took a minute or two, but she finally began to calm down.

"I'm sorry," Tobias whispered, listening for anyone who might have heard the muffled commotion. "I had no choice."

After a few minutes, Charlotte was still. Tobias asked her once more if she would keep quiet, and she nodded. He slowly removed his hands. She shook her head as if she'd just been swimming and needed to shake the water out of her ears.

"Why'd you do that?" Charlotte whimpered, rubbing her arm.

"Sorry," Tobias replied. "I really am, but I need you to think straight."

"I was thinking straight," she protested, still shaking her head. "Who do you think tried to talk you out of that dumb idea?"

"What dumb idea?" Tobias asked.

"To go up to the second floor and . . ." Charlotte stopped and looked around, confused. "Wait a second, what day is it?"

Tobias smiled—his pinching and slamming seemed to have worked.

"I'm not sure. I think it's Friday. They don't have clocks or calendars around here, but I've been making marks under the cot."

Charlotte continued to rub the back of her arm. She reached out and pinched Tobias. "I should smash your toes."

"I'm so glad that worked," he said happily. "So do you remember now?"

"Sort of. We were in the gardens," Charlotte said softly. "And they stopped us, right?"

Tobias nodded.

"We jumped out a window," she said as memories cleared in her mind. "And you stole some pliers."

"And pens," Tobias added. "Then they made us talk to Marvin Withers, and he gummed up our brains."

"In a square room," she said almost reverently.

Tobias nodded.

"I think I was mad at you," Charlotte said. "Really mad."

"You forgave me," Tobias lied.

"I don't remember that part. But I do remember the gardens and Lars and . . . wait! Was there some sort of parade?"

"Kinda. You loved it."

"Everything's coming back. Orrin, Ms. Gulp . . ." Charlotte paused and looked at Tobias. "Dad left us, didn't he?"

"He did." Tobias nodded.

"And Mom's dead," she said in a whisper.

Tobias ached for all the sadness he had been through, but he ached even more for what it had done to his sister.

"I need to sleep," Charlotte said sadly. "I want to wake up somewhere more hopeful."

"If you want to wake up somewhere more hopeful, then we

need to move. They're planning something, an extraction, and if they find out our minds are clear, they'll take us back to old man Withers and dumb us up again with his voice. The only hope we have is to escape NOW!"

Tobias stood and reached for his sister. She breathed in deeply and then took his hand.

"We'll visit Fiddle first."

"Really? He thinks we're made up," Charlotte reminded him.

"Fiddle knows something, and at this hour he should be in his room. He said there was a door that could lead us off the mesa. I think I can get us out of the building, and if he knows where to go from there, then it should be easy."

"Easy?"

"Well, less than impossible." Tobias smiled.

"Plus, I have a surprise for you."

"It's not another pinch, is it?"

Tobias retrieved something from beneath one of the cots.

"My clothes!" Charlotte said with excitement.

He handed Charlotte the clothes she had been wearing when she came to Witherwood.

"When they gave us uniforms, we just left these in the wash-room. And since nobody but us ever goes in there, I hid them in one of the showers."

Charlotte practically squealed. "Turn around and close your eyes."

She changed into her clothes and then kept her eyes shut as Tobias changed into his. They tossed their uniforms with gusto into the corner of their room. It made things seem much more hopeful—Tobias in his red hoodie and Charlotte in her green HOPE shirt.

"Feel better?" Tobias asked.

"Worlds. Let's do this."

Tobias and Charlotte stood at the door and listened for voices. They traveled up the hall to Fiddle's door. Tobias unlocked it.

"What if Fiddle shoots us for sneaking in?"

"At least we won't have to do dishes tomorrow."

That was good enough for Charlotte. Once they were both in the room, Tobias closed the door and turned on the light. The curtains were closed around Fiddle's bed, and they could hear an uneasy sniffling.

"Fiddle?" Tobias said softly. "Fiddle, are you in there?"

There was no reply.

"It's me, Tobias, and my sister, Charlotte."

There was still no reply.

"We were here last week, remember?" Tobias tried.

"Maybe that's not him in there," Charlotte whispered.

"It is. I can smell him."

Tobias stepped carefully toward the bed and pulled back the curtains. Fiddle was lying there with his head resting on his duck-printed pillows. He was wearing a long black nightshirt over shorts and pinching the top of his nose. He smiled at Tobias with his wide mouth.

"Hello, imagination," Fiddle said kindly. "You're back. I guess the lock on my door isn't working?"

"I made a key," Tobias explained.

Fiddle sat up and swung his legs so that they were hanging off the side of the bed. His green eyes sparkled, and his long dark hair appeared even stringier than before. There was a tray of empty plates and glasses at the end of his bed. He pushed the tray back and yawned.

"I like that," he said. "I've got a pretty interesting imagination."

"You didn't make us up," Charlotte insisted.

"I think it's cool how you both have different voices," Fiddle said. "Lots of times my thoughts all sound the same."

"I guess that's cool," Tobias said, pulling at the back of his own hair.

"Actually, I need your help. Would you do me a favor and get me a pen?" Fiddle asked. He pointed at a large chest of drawers near the wall. "Top drawer and hurry, please."

Tobias stepped to the dresser and opened the top drawer. It

was filled with ballpoint pens of all colors and sizes. Tobias took a couple and put them in his pocket. He then grabbed a blue one and brought it back. Instantly Fiddle began to click the top of the pen.

*Click, click, click.*

"Are you going to write something down?" Charlotte asked.

"No," Fiddle said, knitting his eyebrows together. "I'm always surprised how many of the things inside my head are unaware of my problem."

"Problem?" Tobias asked.

"I can't seem to stop fiddling with things," Fiddle said, clicking the pen. "Some doctors call me obsessive compulsive. It's kinda like how you're messing with your hair."

Tobias was immediately embarrassed.

"Not a big deal," Fiddle said in a friendly tone. "You tug your hair, I fiddle with things. That's why they call me what they do— my real name's Clyde."

"I like Fiddle better," Charlotte said.

"Yeah, me too," Fiddle said as he rapidly clicked the top of the pen. "Hey, maybe subconsciously that's why I still do it, just to keep the name. Interesting, I think we've had a real breakthrough here tonight. Of course you two should know more about the condition of my mind, seeing how you came from my thoughts."

*Click, click, click.*

"We came through the door," Charlotte reminded him.

"Fiddle," Tobias said seriously, "we need to talk about something else."

Fiddle closed his eyes and massaged his forehead with his left hand.

After thirty seconds of awkward silence, Tobias asked, "Are you okay?"

"Fine," Fiddle answered. "I was just seeing if I could tell what you were going to say by looking around in my head. Something about the parade?"

"No, although you did a good job sitting on that float."

"Thanks. Actually, they make me participate. My uncle used to sit up there, but he stopped doing that years ago."

"That's great," Tobias said, frustrated. "What I wanted to talk about is when we were last here, you said you knew something about getting off the mesa."

"I did?" Fiddle asked, confused.

"This is going to end badly," Charlotte sighed.

"No, wait." Tobias turned his focus back to Fiddle. "Listen, Fiddle, you said something right before Ms. Gulp took us out—something about a way to get out, something about a door."

"To be honest, I can't remember half the things I say," Fiddle admitted. "But if you really want to get out, just take the tunnel. It has a door on it."

"Tunnel?" Tobias and Charlotte asked in unison.

"Sure," Fiddle said. "It'll take you right down and off the mesa."

"Where is it?" Tobias asked, his heart beginning to race.

"Behind the school. Over by that tree."

"What tree?"

"The one with the crooked branch. Out back behind Witherwood, where the mesa starts to slope downward. Near the spring. It's the tree where that squirrel used to live."

*Click, click, click.*

"Please," Charlotte begged. "Do you think you could stop clicking that pen?"

"Forget the pen," Tobias said. "Can you take us to the tunnel?"

"I don't go out much," he reminded them. "Plus, my uncle told me to stay here."

"Marvin?" Tobias asked.

"Yeah, that's him."

"When did he say that?"

"A couple of years ago," Fiddle answered.

*Click, click, click.*

"Here," Charlotte said anxiously as she pulled an elastic ponytail holder from her skirt pocket. "Can you mess with this instead of that pen? Twist it and pull it, but just stop clicking."

Fiddle looked at the small black band and shrugged. He dropped the pen and immediately began twisting and stretching Charlotte's hair tie.

"Do you ever listen to the voices in your head?" Tobias asked.

"Sometimes," Fiddle admitted.

"Well, this voice is telling you to take us to that tunnel," Tobias said.

"We can't get out of the building," Fiddle reminded them. "They chain the outer doors at night."

"I think I know a way."

Fiddle smiled. "I forgot about my great imagination. It looks like I've thought of everything."

"Yes," Charlotte said. "You've been a tremendous help."

"I really have," Fiddle agreed.

The hallway was empty, and there were no singing voices. The three of them crept quietly in the direction of the kitchen. While creeping, Fiddle asked if they were helping him or if he was helping them. Charlotte laughed in the way that someone might laugh when she discovers she has gotten a flat tire or lost some money, more out of frustration than humor.

"There's no way this is going to work," she said.

Fiddle looked down at her and smiled. "You're like the negative part of my imagination."

Charlotte wanted to reply, but the only things she could think to say were negative. Tobias spoke for her.

"She's just reminding us that it's going to take a bit of luck to make this work."

"Well then, I'll wish for a bit of luck. I like adventure, even though I know my uncle wouldn't approve of this."

"Good," Tobias said. "That probably means we're on the right course."

They walked down the hall toward the kitchen as they proceeded on the right or, quite possibly, the wrong course.

# CHAPTER 20

# THE SQUIRREL TREE

Witherwood seemed guarded and afraid. It felt as if the walls were coiling in tighter to protect whatever it was the school was hiding.

"Tell me if you hear anything," Tobias said to Charlotte.

"It's raining outside."

"I can smell that."

"It sounds like the hall is empty for the moment," she added. "I can hear voices singing, but they seem to be in the other halls and growing distant."

"Good. As long as they believe we're still under the spell of Marvin's voice, they won't expect us to escape."

Fiddle kept his head down and moved with a catlike stealth as he followed Tobias and Charlotte. They passed the large double doors that led out behind the school. As expected, the doors were secured with chains.

"Are you doing okay?" Tobias whispered to Fiddle.

"Silly imagination. You know I am. I'm actually having a way better time than I thought I would tonight."

They walked through Weary Hall and turned into Never Hall, where the cathedral-like cafeteria was. The lights were off. The place was empty and still.

"Come on," Tobias said.

He led Charlotte and Fiddle to the kitchen and down into the cellar. Tobias grabbed a small flashlight that Ms. Gulp used when she was down there. They followed the large pipes that ran to the back of the cellar and up out of Witherwood. Where the pipes exited the building was a set of stone stairs that looked as if they led directly into the ceiling. Only it wasn't the ceiling. It was two metal doors that were used for deliveries. The sound of rain falling against the doors was almost calming; the sight of a chain twisting through the door handles was not. A padlock dangled from the chain like some sort of metallic mistletoe that people were supposed to cry under.

Tobias didn't cry—he swore. As far as swear words go, it wasn't the worst one in the world, but it had bite to it. "I was hoping they didn't padlock these doors. I thought they'd forget the cellar. It's never chained in the day."

"This was your escape plan?" Charlotte asked. "You know that they secure all the doors at night. They're trying to keep us in, remember?"

"Technically, that's not true," Fiddle said. "They're trying to keep things out."

"That's just what they tell everyone to keep us in here," Tobias insisted.

Charlotte climbed the stairs to inspect the lock. Her brother had been the one to open locks before, but now it was her turn. Holding the padlock next to her right ear, she twisted the old dial clockwise.

"Can you hear that?" she asked.

"No," the boys answered.

Charlotte turned the lock some more. "You can't hear that click?"

They shook their heads this time.

"My hearing has gotten so much stronger since I've been here," Charlotte said in disbelief. She turned the lock a few more times and then, with one quick jerk, she pulled the padlock open.

"Nice!" Tobias whispered.

It's interesting how everyone has different gifts. You might be remarkable at guessing people's weight, or perhaps you're a gifted whistler, or maybe you're just a supertalented TV watcher. Good for you. It's important to note, however, that Tobias's and Charlotte's abilities to smell and hear were becoming more superpowers than gifts. They were good at other things, but something about Witherwood was making their senses otherworldly.

Charlotte unwrapped the chain from around the handles and set it on the stone stairs. The chain was off, but the delivery doors were still locked. Tobias tried his key, but the lock was different than the others in Witherwood.

"I need a knife or something."

"That would take too long," Fiddle said. "Move aside."

Fiddle ran up the stairs, and with all his strength, he threw his right shoulder into the doors. The old lock popped, and the doors flew open like metal wings.

All three of them climbed the stairs and stepped out into the open. White stones lay scattered all over, glowing in the night like Easter eggs that had been forgotten. Tobias looked up at the back side of Witherwood while his sister looked out into the dark grounds behind it. There were a few other buildings and more trees than in the gardens.

"Do you still know where the tunnel door is?" Tobias asked Fiddle.

"I do."

"Wait," Charlotte said, worried. "I'm not sure we should go out there. Remember what was in front of the school?"

"I know. We'll have to move fast," Tobias said. "Let's just hope all the animals are at the front."

"They're not," Fiddle said. "They're all over the mesa."

"Are you trying to scare us?" Charlotte asked.

"No," Fiddle said casually. "It's funny that my imagination is worried about animals. It's always been the Catchers that concern me most."

"Catchers?" Tobias asked with extreme curiosity.

"Yeah, they bring the students here," Fiddle answered. "But don't worry about that now. I don't think anyone will care about my imagination wandering off."

Charlotte stared at Fiddle, worried about him almost as much as herself.

"I don't understand," Tobias whispered. "Catchers? What are they? Nobody caught us."

"Sure," Fiddle said. "You're not real."

"But there is a tunnel, right?" Charlotte asked.

"I didn't realize I was so doubtful," Fiddle said, staring at Charlotte. "Yes, there's a tunnel. Come on."

Rain danced on their hair and shoulders as they walked. They passed three smaller buildings that looked abandoned. Beyond those buildings were more trees. The air smelled like cedar.

"There's the first outhouse," Fiddle said happily.

Charlotte eww'd.

"I didn't know there was all this land in the back," Tobias said.

"Well, there is. The mesa's over a mile wide on top and at least as long. It begins to slope here. If you walk straight, you'll reach the back fence in about half a mile."

"So is that where we're going?" Tobias asked.

"Nope. We're going to the spring."

Charlotte stopped. She grabbed her brother's arm.

"What is it?" Tobias asked.

"I can hear something. Look, there!"

Charlotte motioned to a small, dark shadow on the ground behind them. She bent down to look closer.

The shadow moved.

"I wouldn't go touching things," Fiddle warned.

The small shadow leaped into Charlotte's arms.

"Lars!" she exclaimed.

Tobias shined the flashlight on the creature. It shivered in his sister's arms and blinked slowly at her as if it was glad to see her.

"You have a weird connection with animals," Tobias said.

Lars began making an odd clicking purr.

"I'm bringing him," Charlotte informed them while tying the front hem of her shirt to create a pouch.

"I'm not going to stop you," Tobias said.

"I just think it's really nice of my imagination to care about animals," Fiddle said sincerely. "I must be a good person."

"You are," Tobias said. "Now show us the way out of here."

Fiddle stepped off the small dirt trail they were on and headed straight into the trees. Tobias tried to keep the beam of the flashlight in front of Fiddle. The trees grew thicker and then thinned as the terrain became rockier.

Charlotte stopped and listened for a moment. "Something else is following us."

Tobias glanced back into the dark night. "What is it?"

"I'm not sure, but it's bigger than Lars."

"It's probably one of the Protectors," Fiddle answered.

"Protectors?" Tobias asked.

"The animals that guard Witherwood," Fiddle said, twisting the hair tie. "One of those creatures that hurt that tall girl years ago."

Tobias and Charlotte stared at each other.

"Well then, go faster," Tobias begged.

Fiddle picked up the pace.

"I hate this," Charlotte said. "My heart's beating like mad."

They ran about a hundred feet farther before coming to the edge of a small stream.

"We're going to get a little wet," Fiddle informed them. He then stepped down the rocky bank and waded in. "The sides of the stream are thick with thornbushes. We need to head back up the stream to get to the start of it. Let's hope walking in the water keeps some of the animals away."

Tobias and Charlotte followed Fiddle. All three walked up the stream. The movement of water seemed to match the flood of worry and fear they had in their guts.

Heading upstream, they could see small bits of the back side of Witherwood. A couple of windows lit up, and a piercing alarm began to scream. Witherwood was like a giant ogre waking to the knowledge of them running away.

"You better be right about this," Charlotte chastised Tobias while holding Lars tightly.

"I really hope I am," he replied, sounding less confident than he wanted to.

After about one hundred feet of pushing through water, they were stopped by a thicket of trees growing out over the stream. The water appeared to burst right out from under the trees.

"There it is," Fiddle said.

Tobias directed the flashlight's beam at the spot where the water emerged from the trees.

"It's behind those," Fiddle reported.

"Wait," Charlotte said urgently. "You should turn off the flashlight."

Tobias shut off his light. Hundreds of white stones glowed all around them. Downstream they could see a dark shape coming

closer, and back by the school, there were four flashlights bobbing.

"We need to move faster," Charlotte whispered.

Fiddle led Tobias and Charlotte through the trees and then pushed himself between a fat bush and two skinny tree trunks. Tobias and Charlotte twisted and bent their bodies trying to keep up with him.

"There's that tree I was talking about," Fiddle said proudly.

They could see the huge tree Fiddle had described. It was almost three stories tall, with a trunk as thick as an oil drum. It had multiple branches, and one of them was bent down and touching the water.

"That's weird," Fiddle whispered.

"What's weird?"

"I remember there being a squirrel in that tree."

"Just go," Tobias insisted.

Fiddle pushed aside the huge hanging branch, exposing a large gash in the ground from which the spring poured forth.

"Is that what you meant by tunnel?" Tobias asked in a panic. "Because there's no way we could crawl up in there with that water rushing out."

"No," Fiddle said. "You're really not my smartest imagination."

Fiddle pulled the branch back even farther, uncovering a concrete slab with a round metal hatch set into it.

"Not many people know this is here," Fiddle said. "But I do. I've been through it a couple of times. Years ago, they used it to sneak stuff in."

Fiddle grabbed hold of the latch on top of the small door and tried to slide it open. It was rusted stuck. "I don't think anyone's used it in a while."

"Move back," Tobias said, waving him away.

The sound of something large splashing into the stream motivated Tobias to raise his right foot and kick the latch as hard as he could. It squeaked and whined and then, with one sharp click, it miraculously opened.

"Hurry," Charlotte said, looking back. "Hurry!"

Tobias and Fiddle pulled the round door open, and hundreds of bats shot out into the sky. They slapped up against the children's faces and caused all three to scream in ways that weren't very dignified. Lars did some screaming of his own. One bat tangled in Charlotte's hair, and Tobias had to swat it out. As the bats cleared, they could hear splashing in the water not far behind them.

"Something's here!" Charlotte said.

Tobias looked at his sister and went as pale as the moon. There, standing in the water just a few feet away, was a creature as tall as Tobias. It had long, leathery arms and a round body with quills covering most of its torso. Its head looked like a wolf with twisted ears, and it was snarling. The animal's eyes opened and closed slowly as the smell of something rotten filled the air.

"If that's real, we're in trouble," Fiddle said in awe.

The creature lunged and slipped on the wet ground. As it tried to find its footing, Tobias pushed Fiddle, Charlotte, and Lars through the hatch door and slammed it behind him. He hooked the lock, but it wouldn't stay closed.

The creature outside wasn't happy. It scratched and screamed at the hatch as if its life depended on getting in. Charlotte grabbed the flashlight from Tobias. She lit up her brother as he held the door and she held Lars.

"It won't stay shut unless I hold it!" Tobias yelled. "The latch is busted!"

"I'll do it," Fiddle said. "You two go."

"No way," Tobias argued.

"You have to," Fiddle said almost excitedly. "I don't know if you're real or my imagination. Actually, I'm pretty sure I'm making this all up—I mean, the things I've seen. How can any of it be true? But I'd kinda like to see what would happen if some of my thoughts got out of this place. So run that way." Fiddle pointed down the tunnel. "You'll find stairs. Follow them all the way down. There will be a fork in the tunnel. Take the right one. Just past the fork, the tunnel will slope downward. Keep going, and when it levels out, run for about a mile more. Then you'll bump into a

door. It'll feel like a long run, but the door will be there. Open it and you're free."

The creature outside of the hatch shrieked. Fiddle pushed Tobias aside and held the latch in place.

"What about you?" Charlotte asked.

"People from the school will come," Fiddle said, sweating slightly. "And daylight will put the Protectors to sleep."

"But if they come from the school, they'll catch you," Charlotte said, stating the obvious.

"Big deal." Fiddle laughed. "They can't stop me from imagining. Besides, I'm a Withers. My uncle won't hurt me. Now go."

"We're coming back for you," Tobias insisted.

"I'd like that. This is the most fun I've had in a while."

"Thanks, Fiddle," Charlotte said.

"Anytime," he replied as the Protector angrily screamed outside the hatch.

Tobias and Charlotte took off, running down the cement tunnel as fast as they could. After a hundred feet they came to a downward spiral staircase. When the stairs finally ended, there was more tunnel. Charlotte jumped out ahead, and Tobias followed.

"Remember where we're going!" Tobias yelled. "In case we get lost down here."

"Why?" Charlotte asked. "It's not like I'm ever heading back. Did you see that animal?"

"I don't want to think about it."

It was a wise thing for Tobias to say. If you had seen what he just saw, you too would probably choose not to think about it. It was one thing for Witherwood to have cruel staff members and troublesome classes. There was nothing comforting about a forbidden third floor or a second floor that looks like a hospital. No recruiting brochure would list Marvin's voice or the square room as an attraction. No, Witherwood was a place of great misunderstanding and concern, but all those concerns were made worse by the knowledge that beasts like the Protectors roamed the top of the mesa.

Tobias and Charlotte picked up the pace. The tunnel was filled with cobwebs. Every few feet, they would twist through a huge web and then have to peel it off as they ran. Two stray bats flew past them.

They came to the fork in the tunnel and stayed to the right, just as Fiddle had said. Behind them there was a feeling of dread, but ahead there was a growing feeling of hope. Lars clicked and purred as they ran.

# CHAPTER 21

# REST STOP

Tobias and Charlotte had no idea how far they had run, but they were done with it. The flashlight had stopped working, and now there was nothing but darkness. They had run until the cement tunnel started sloping downward. Then they had run until it finally leveled out. After that, their running turned into a slow jog. Eventually, that slow jog became a weary shuffle. And now they were simply begging their feet to keep moving forward any way possible.

"Are you sure this is the right tunnel?" Charlotte asked, her body almost completely broken down from everything she had been through.

"I only know what Fiddle said," Tobias reminded her.

"I don't think I can go any farther," Charlotte pleaded. "And Lars is getting heavy."

"What does he weigh—three pounds? We can't stop now. We're almost out."

"What if Fiddle was wrong? He said go down the right tunnel. What if he got his directions messed up?"

"He's not wrong."

"He doesn't even think we really exist."

"We'll go a little more and then rest."

They shuffled silently for a few minutes before Charlotte spoke up. "Why is this happening? I thought when Mom died that would be the worst moment of my life, but now look at us."

"It's too dark to see us," Tobias tried to joke.

"It's not funny," Charlotte reminded him.

Tobias sighed. "You're right. This is ridiculous. But you know what?"

"What?"

"The one thing that hasn't stunk this entire time is that you were here. I don't know what I would have done if they had split us up, or if I had been alone."

"Really?" Charlotte asked, surprised by her brother's compliment.

"Honest," Tobias said.

Just then he ran into a hard wall. He bounced back and fell onto Charlotte, taking them both down. Lars squawked.

"What happened?" Charlotte asked.

"I hit something."

They scrambled to their feet and began feeling around in the dark.

"It's a door," Charlotte yelled. "IT'S A DOOR!"

Tobias could feel a long board on the front of the door. He lifted it and slid it out of the brackets it was resting in. He pushed the door open and bits of moonlight drifted in. They both stepped out and noticed a row of toilets, a few sinks, and some broken windows. Bird droppings were everywhere, and a startled bird shot from beneath a bathroom stall and flew out one of the windows.

"What is this place?" Charlotte asked. "We're out, right? We're not still in Witherwood, are we?"

"No way," Tobias insisted. "This isn't Witherwood."

Tobias walked up to one of the sinks and turned the faucet handle—no water. He looked out a window and could see a road.

"I think we're at some old rest stop," he said.

Charlotte walked over to the front door and easily slid back the lock. "Good. I'd hate to be stuck in a bathroom the rest of my life."

Tobias smiled, his heart lighter than it had been in a long time. Charlotte pushed the door open, and they walked on the uneven sidewalk at the edge of an overgrown parking lot. It was dark, and the clouds were beginning to move across the moon.

"We did it," Tobias said in amazement.

"I can't believe—" Charlotte started to say. Her slightly pointed ears began to twitch. "Wait, do you hear that?"

The sound of a car grew louder. The car turned off the road and pulled up in front of them, its headlights shining into their eyes.

"Who's that?" Charlotte whispered.

"How would I know?" Tobias said nervously.

"Should we run?"

"Not yet."

They couldn't see the driver due to the blinding headlights, but they could hear a car door open and the sound of someone stepping out.

"Who's there?" Tobias yelled. "Don't come any closer."

"I'm Sheriff Pidge," a friendly voice hollered back. "Are you two okay?"

Tobias and Charlotte looked at each other.

"We made it!" they both said together.

Charlotte smiled and Tobias cheered while Lars did nothing but purr.

## CHAPTER 22

# HOPE

*Go ahead and close this book. It might be fun to pretend that everything ends just how you want it to. The Eggers kids are saved—why ruin the mood? If, however, you choose to continue, please don't complain about not being forewarned.*

*And so it goes....*

Tobias and Charlotte climbed into the back of the cop car with wide smiles on their faces.

"Watch your heads," Sheriff Pidge said kindly. "I need to get you home in good condition. Well, no worse condition."

Tobias and Charlotte looked at Sheriff Pidge and laughed.

Sheriff Pidge was a medium-sized man with uneven shoulders

and a tiny waist. He was wearing a full sheriff's uniform, including a stiff brown hat and a gun on his belt. He had a thin mustache and a friendly smile. The two had told him all they had been through since their father had dropped them off. They told him about the animals and showed him Lars. They told him about Orrin, Ms. Gulp, Mr. Himzakity, the dishes, the drudgery, the secret floors, and Student Morale Day. Sheriff Pidge had written down some notes and radioed his station the information.

The sheriff shut the car door for Tobias and then climbed into the driver's seat. He adjusted his rearview mirror to get a better look at the kids.

"Ready to go home?" he said with a wink.

"Yes," Tobias said with enthusiasm.

"What a relief," Charlotte said as Lars settled on her lap.

Sheriff Pidge started the car and pulled out of the overgrown parking lot onto the highway.

"I've never been in a cop car before," Tobias said, looking at Charlotte. "I always thought it would be a bad thing. But I'm pretty happy to be in one now."

"Me too. I can't wait to see Dad."

"Same here. I have a few questions for him."

The back seats in the squad car were made out of a hard

plastic and were not very comfortable. There was a metal screen dividing them from Sheriff Pidge.

"I can't wait to sleep in a real bed, with pillows." Charlotte looked out the rear window. Her ears twitched again. She turned to look out the front and then looked back again.

Tobias watched her expression grow grim, and a weird feeling began to creep up the back of his spine. Something wasn't right. He searched his brain for any indication of what that something might be.

"Sheriff?" Tobias called out.

"Yes?" he replied.

"How did you know we were there?" Tobias asked through the screen.

"I didn't," Sheriff Pidge said as he continued to drive. "Just luck, I guess. I check that abandoned rest stop every now and then to see if anyone's in there messing around. Imagine my surprise when I found two kids."

"Oh," Tobias said uncomfortably.

Charlotte pinched her brother softly. "I think we're going in the wrong direction," she whispered in a panic.

At that moment, Sheriff Pidge turned off the highway and onto the twisty road. There, like a horrible ugly villain, sat the large Witherwood sign.

"WHAT ARE YOU DOING?"

"Calm yourselves," Sheriff Pidge said coolly. "If what you say is true about how bad this place is, I need to check it out."

"NO!" Tobias shouted. "If you're going anywhere near Witherwood, let us out."

"I don't think that's a good idea," Sheriff Pidge said. "I mean, your dad left you out here, and look what happened."

"Let us out," Charlotte demanded. "We're not going back in there!"

"I beg to differ," the sheriff replied. "I promised I'd take you home, didn't I?"

Tobias and Charlotte frantically tried the doors, but they were locked. Charlotte started to pound on the metal screen, while Tobias shifted and kicked at the side window with his feet. Lars kept quiet.

Sheriff Pidge paid no attention. He just pressed on the gas and zoomed up the twisty road to the top of the mesa.

"You can't do this!" Tobias hollered. "There's something awful going on in that school!"

"I don't think it will hurt you two to do a few dishes," Sheriff Pidge said, smiling. "Witherwood is a trusted institution."

"I'm not talking about dishes," Tobias hollered. "There's something really weird happening in there—something wrong."

"What?" Sheriff Pidge asked. "What's so wrong?"

"There's animals and strange-smelling pudding and awful parades and a forbidden third floor and—"

"If you ask me," the sheriff interrupted Tobias, "that animal looks friendly. And I think Witherwood is an important place of learning, and you should realize how fortunate you are to be a student."

"We're not going back," Charlotte snapped.

Tobias continued to kick at the window, but the thick glass was showing no signs of breaking. He shifted again and began to claw at the door, looking for some way to open it.

"Good luck," Sheriff Pidge said, glancing back at them through his rearview mirror. "Cop cars are designed to keep you in. Sort of like Witherwood, I suppose."

Tobias and Charlotte yelled and screamed and pleaded, but the sheriff just ignored them. The road leveled out, and in the beams of the headlights, the foreboding iron gate appeared.

"I can't believe this," Charlotte said desperately, beginning to hyperventilate. "We were out!"

Sheriff Pidge reached up and pressed a garage door opener that was clipped to his visor. The iron gate began to beep and open.

"You have a remote to the gate?" Tobias asked in disgust. "You weren't checking the rest stop—you were hunting for us!"

"When my uncle Marvin calls and asks for a favor, I do it. He's family, and what kind of a world would it be if people stopped helping family?"

Charlotte was so exhausted, all she could do was cry.

The car moved slowly along the cobblestone drive. The first signs of daylight were beginning to appear. Tobias gazed out his window and stared at the odd trees, wondering if he would ever feel safe again.

# CHAPTER 23

# THE LOOKING GLASS

heriff Pidge escorted Tobias and Charlotte into the office. An orderly took Lars from Charlotte, and they were taken by Orrin and Ms. Gulp through the school and back to the ivy-covered building in the center of the gardens. They begged to be let go, or to be sent to their room, or to the kitchen to clean—anything but back to Marvin. They both knew if they heard his voice, there was a good chance they would never think clearly again.

"Don't do this," Tobias pleaded.

"We would have preferred you stay in your room and not try to escape," Orrin said. "But you didn't. This is for your own good."

"I told you both to do as you're told and nothing else," Ms. Gulp reminded them.

"We'll stay put now," Charlotte tried to assure them.

"It's too late for that," Orrin said sadly.

It felt too late. They had blown it. Clearly, they should have run from Sheriff Pidge.

Ms. Gulp opened the front door to the square building, and Orrin pushed them in. The door slammed behind them. They flopped into the chairs, completely deflated. In the mirror, they could see the words that were painted on the wall behind them: *Time is a trick of the mind.*

Tobias put his head in his hands and spoke. "We need Dad. I know he didn't mean for this to happen. I don't care if he grounds me for a year, or has me do chores forever, or if he wants me to apologize to Martha. I'll do it. I want to go home."

The light in the square room suddenly dimmed, and the mirror began to glow.

"Cover your ears," Tobias commanded.

They both put their hands up over their ears.

"Hello," the familiar voice spoke.

Tobias and Charlotte just sat there looking like something the cat had not only dragged in but had chewed on and scratched at for hours. They had their ears covered; still, Marvin's voice was as clear as if they didn't. It permeated their minds and souls. Both of them dropped their hands, realizing it was futile. Tobias stood up.

"Yes," Marvin said. "Many have tried to cover their ears. It seems my voice has a way of sneaking in."

Charlotte stood next to her brother.

"I didn't think I would see you two again so soon. Such a strong desire to leave us. Tell me, why are you so desperate to flee?"

Tobias and Charlotte stared at the glowing mirror. There was no sign of the silhouette or image of Marvin behind it yet.

"We don't belong here," Tobias tried. "Just let us go."

"But why?" Marvin asked, his words drifting down on them like snow. "Your father left you, and now you are fortunate to have this home."

"This is not our home," Tobias insisted.

"How wrong you are," Marvin said. "I didn't tell him to drop you off. In fact, it is a burden to us to have to care for you. Food, shelter, education, safety—those things aren't free."

"Thank you," Charlotte said. Marvin's voice was already messing her head up.

"However, we make those sacrifices so that we always have just the right students," Marvin said with a syrupy voice. "The science we perform here requires a certain type of child."

"What?" Tobias asked, not understanding what Marvin was saying.

"I'm always surprised how the Catchers manage to find just the right ones," Marvin answered. "You children who come to us in nontraditional ways are always more of a risk. But your strong spirit is going to produce quite the prize someday. Now, why don't you just relax and listen to my voice. We're glad to have you back."

Tobias shivered.

"Listen," Marvin said as the room continued to grow darker and the mirror brighter. "This is a reform school, and you will be changed."

"Our dad will find us," Tobias insisted, his brain trying desperately to fight off the oncoming fog.

"Yes," Marvin said. "About that. I think there's something you should see."

There was a long pause, followed by the sound of something moving behind the glass.

"What does he want us to see?" Charlotte asked.

"I'm pretty sure it won't be good."

Charlotte shook her head. "I can already feel my brain going dumb."

"Yeah, I could tell when you thanked him for taking care of us."

The room became completely bright, and the mirrored wall no longer glowed at the edges. A light snapped on behind the mirror,

and they could see right through and into the space behind it. There was nothing on the other side besides the empty leather chair and a back door.

"Where's Marvin?" Tobias asked.

Before Charlotte could answer, the back door behind the mirror opened and Orrin walked in. He was just as short as he had always been, but he wore a smile that suggested he was hiding something.

"What's he doing?" Charlotte asked.

Orrin stood there for a second, staring at the Eggers kids with his mismatched eyes. He was wearing his white overcoat, and his four gray hairs were combed over and plastered to his head. He scratched himself and grinned. Behind him, coming through the door, was Ralph Eggers. Their father had his arm in a cast and a troubled look on his face.

"Dad!" Tobias and Charlotte shouted. "Dad!"

The two children ran to the mirror and began to pound on it. Ralph Eggers spun and looked at them. He stepped back, frightened by their appearance and actions.

"Dad!" Charlotte hollered. "It's us."

They could see Orrin saying something to their father but couldn't hear him. Orrin pointed toward Tobias and Charlotte, and Ralph looked at them and shook his head sadly.

"Dad," Charlotte pleaded.

Tobias bent down and picked up a chair. He threw it at the mirror, but it did nothing except frighten Ralph more.

"Dad!" Tobias screamed.

Orrin and Mr. Eggers turned away from them and walked out the back door of the square room.

"I don't get what's happening," Charlotte cried. "Dad!"

Tobias ran to the trapdoor in the middle of the floor. He grabbed the gold ring and pulled—it was still locked tight. He ran to the front door and desperately tried to open it. He pounded and yelled.

"Dad! Dad!"

Charlotte fell to her knees with her head in her hands as she and her big brother let go of every bit of hope they had ever held in their lives.

It was not a pleasant feeling.

# CHAPTER 24

# ABHORRENCE

*People are easily startled. It's a fact that's simple to prove. Walk up behind someone with a pin and a balloon, and you'll see for yourself. Or if you're feeling really adventurous, procure two thin flat boards and when someone is sleeping, slap the boards together as hard as you can. It's a fun way to make friends.*

R alph Eggers was more startled by what he had just seen than if someone had slapped two boards together right next to his ear. He left the square building no wiser than when he had entered.

"So," Sam said to Ralph as he came out with Orrin, "did you see anything familiar?"

"No," Ralph answered, confused. "Just a couple of kids."

"What'd they say?" Sam asked.

"We couldn't hear them," Ralph replied. "They seemed out of control."

"The two-way mirror is soundproof when we need it to be," Orrin said. "I didn't want you to hear some of the vulgar things they were saying. Those two kids are a couple of our tougher cases. We love them all, but some are just a bit more challenging than others. I wanted you to see what we're working with here. I'm pretty certain you would have remembered being around that. Is there anything else we can do for you?"

Ralph shook his head. "It looks like this is a dead end."

Ralph, Sam, and Orrin walked through the gardens in silence. At the front of the school, Sam got into the driver's seat of his taxi while Ralph thanked Orrin.

"I wish we could have helped," Orrin said.

"So do I. Before I go, do you mind if I ask you one last question?"

"Please," Orrin said, looking up at Ralph. "Anything."

"You don't happen to know anyone by the name of Martha here?"

"There's no one here named that," Orrin answered.

Ralph shrugged, looked at Witherwood one last time, then got into the taxi, and Sam drove away.

# CHAPTER 25

# GLIMMER

Tobias and Charlotte shuffled down the hall with Ms. Gulp behind them. After their father had disappeared, they had spent the next two hours in the square room listening to Marvin and forgetting everything. Their brains were so mucked up now that they couldn't even remember seeing their dad.

"We've put a new lock on your door," Ms. Gulp said, creaking as they walked through Weary Hall. "Our security needed an update. Things should stay where they are now."

"What about when we need to use the bathroom?" Charlotte asked kindly.

"I still find your questions insufferable," Ms. Gulp said, bothered. "There will be someone checking on you every couple of hours to make sure you're still in your beds. Ask them to take you."

"That's nice," Tobias said. "Thank you so much."

"It looks like Marvin really got to you," Ms. Gulp said, smiling. "I don't know why he doesn't just forget about you two. But I suppose he's always in need of new things to . . . well . . ."

"What?" Charlotte asked.

Ms. Gulp stopped walking and turned to face them. With a cruel smile, she said, "What I meant was that I suppose there's value in everyone."

"I'm glad we can help," Charlotte said.

When they reached the seventh door on the left, Ms. Gulp took out a black key and unlocked the new lock. She pushed Tobias and Charlotte inside their room.

"You might want to rest up," Ms. Gulp growled. "Come morning, you'll be working harder than ever."

"Okay," Tobias and Charlotte said in a pleasant way. "We will."

"And remember, do as you're told and not a thing more."

Ms. Gulp slammed the door and locked it. Tobias and Charlotte stood there blinking slowly and trying to figure out how they should feel.

"It seems like we should be talking about something important," Tobias said to his sister.

"Really?" Charlotte said, walking to her cot. "What do you think we should be talking about?"

"I can't remember," Tobias told her.

*Now, I know what you're probably thinking: "I can't remember" wasn't really the best line of dialogue to end the book on. But the future for Tobias and Charlotte wasn't going to be easy. They were trapped in Witherwood, and it appeared that even their father had abandoned them. It certainly seemed like a moment when it would have been nice to see hope come pouring down on them in buckets. Instead, however, hope came in a thimble.*

At the head of both their cots were two large pillows with duck-print pillowcases. Somehow, Fiddle had made it back and delivered them something hopeful. They didn't know this, or even remember Fiddle, but they knew what pillows were and they were happy to see them.

Tobias almost cried. Charlotte started to whimper with joy as she sat down on her cot, leaned back, and let her head sink into the pillow. Tobias took a second to slip off his shoes and then did exactly the same.

In the moments before he drifted into a foggy sleep, Tobias noticed the floor beneath one of the empty cots. The way the light rested on the dusty surface was most unusual. Something about it made Tobias hopeful.

He closed his eyes and let sleep smother him.

These were small things—a map written in the dust, pillows to rest their heads on—but it's amazing how far a tiny thimble of hope and ten hours of sleep can go toward making things right.

TO BE CONTINUED...

# I Might Add

Some people will shut this book and talk about how children are best kept locked up in mysterious schools high on a mesa that grew from a meteor that fell in the middle of a desert. Some will shut it and talk about how parents should be careful when they punish their kids—they'll say Ralph should have just sent them to their room or made them clean up the house instead of what he did. And some readers will simply shut the book and remember to check what's in the gravy before they eat it next time.

What Tobias and Charlotte have learned is that their ordeal is just beginning. Sure, people don't always ask to be taught, and some of us are reluctant to learn anything at all, but what lies ahead for Tobias and Charlotte is going to wise them up, whether they like it or not. Yes, I'm afraid that great changes are still in store. And even though life is pinching them hard, you can take comfort in the fact that it's not you. Of course, if Tobias and Charlotte don't find a way to bring down Witherwood, it very well could be you someday.

# WITHERWOOD
# REFORM SCHOOL

### ⇌ BOOK 2 ⇋

# LOST AND FOUND

## COMING SOON!

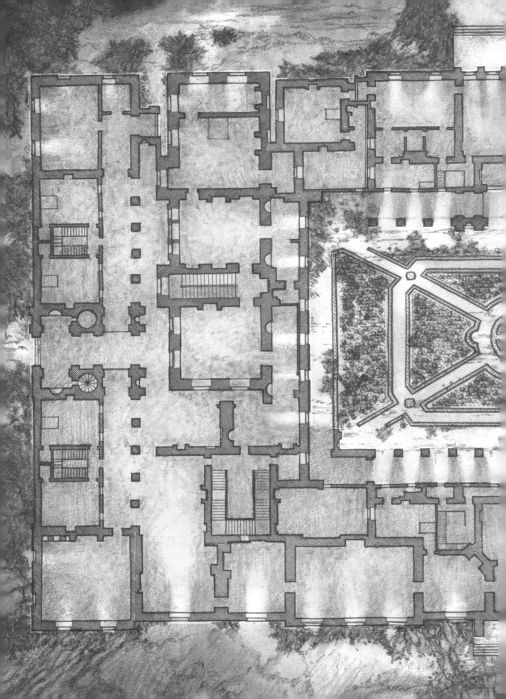